AMANDA, I HOPE YOU
ENJOY THE STORY.

DAD

Adventures
of the *Black Duck*

Written by Vince Pisani

PublishAmerica
Baltimore

First printing

This is a work of fiction. Names, characters, places, and incidents either are the product of the author's imagination or are used fictitiously. Any resemblance to actual persons, living or dead, events, or locales is entirely coincidental

ISBN: 1-4241-7363-9
PUBLISHED BY PUBLISHAMERICA, LLLP
www.publishamerica.com
Baltimore

Printed in the United States of America

To my mother, Angie, who raised me to believe in myself and that you can accomplish anything if you put your mind to it.

To my son, Michael, who, during the summer of 2004 at the age of eleven, endured a 2000-mile trip on the back of my motorcycle from New Jersey to Nova Scotia and back while doing research for this book.

To my daughter, Amanda, who opened my eyes and made me believe I can write.

And lastly, to my dear friend Ed Zolla, who left us unexpectedly in September of 2006. Ed provided me with the resources, wisdom and inspiration to reach for the stars and to pursue my dreams.

Acknowledgements

I would like to acknowledge and thank the following people for their support and encouragement.

Sue Hercock, an English teacher at Rancocas Valley Regional High School, for reading the original five pages and encouraging me to continue writing my story. To Donna Danato, a teacher at Eastern High School, who told me, after reading the first fifteen chapters, the story was very interesting and she wanted to know how it ended. Pat Lopresti, who provided me the basic skills I needed to write my manuscript. To Claire Cohen, who encouraged me to finish the manuscript. To Dr. Stan Cohen, who assisted me in my search for a publisher. In addition, I would like to thank my family, friends and colleagues, who so patiently waited for me to complete this book.

Prologue

Life as I know it began in the summer of nineteen seventy-six. Disco was the latest craze; "dancing the night away" really had true meaning. I had just graduated high school with no intention of going to college. Everyone I grew up with dreamt only of a higher education but for me it would be off to work. I had been working since I was twelve years old so it really didn't matter if I graduated or not. Work was going to be a way of life, for what I thought at the time would be the rest of my life.

I was born in late October so I graduated younger than the rest of my class and friends. Being seventeen and out of school with a diploma seemed to be cool, especially since I graduated in the top of my class. Everyone said I had lots of potential but for me girls, bars, and work were the only things on my mind. I wasn't legally old enough to go to bars but managed to get in anyway. At the time it was the only place I thought I could meet girls.

One day a group of friends asked me to meet them at a bar called The Black Duck. No disco would ever play there. This was a real bar with character. A group of kids, because that's all we really were, would meet there Saturday nights to escape the disco scene and do some serious drinking. The bar sat on a barge moored under the highway bridge in a secluded section of town. I was into dancing so I never even thought of going there, plus I never considered myself a serious drinker.

I arrived early in the evening to check the place out and avoid the wait in line to get in. The Black Duck was not a big place, by any stretch of the imagination, so I thought getting there early was a smart move. When I arrived, the sun was still out. I worked on Saturdays 'til three in the afternoon, and by the time I finished work my friends had already disappeared for the day, or at least 'til the sun went down. I went up to the bar and ordered my usual drink, Molson, a Canadian beer, a true beer drinker's beer, not too light, not too dark; just right.

As I looked around, there were only a few patrons in the bar. I pulled up a stool and watched NASCAR racing on the TV above the bar. NASCAR started to become big business. Companies like the RJ Reynolds Tobacco Company and Busch Beer were huge sponsors. Women were also starting to watch the sport and these sponsors were going to capitalize on the growing market. After a few beers, I asked where the men's room was. The bartender said, "At the end of the bar and turn left." I strolled down to take care of business and noticed an old man sitting by himself just staring around. I thought he was just a local lush, as they were called in those days, so I just walked around his table.

When I returned to the barroom, I couldn't help but notice the old man's rough look. Growing up in New England and living near the ocean made it easy to spot a salty dog a mile away. You could see by the look of him he had more character than the bar and had certainly lived on the ocean.

As I passed the old man, I thought I heard him say something to me. He was mumbling something about the NASCAR drivers on the TV. He said something like, "If it wasn't for me none of you would be making it big, you'd all be in jail." Since I was alone and had started to catch a little buzz, I pulled up a chair and invited myself to sit with him. I ordered another drink from the bar and decided to chat with the old man 'til my friends showed up. I was always one who could strike up a conversation with anyone about anything. But for some reason, I had a feeling this salty dog wasn't going to be just "anyone," or talk about just "anything."

He had a whiskey in front of him, which he had milked for a while. Not wanting him to get kicked out of the bar, I ordered him a fresh drink. The old man thanked me politely and asked why I bought him the drink. I said, "You look like you've been around the block a few times, so for the price of a whiskey, what advice can you give someone who just graduated high school with no real direction in life?" He spoke a few words under his breath, which I couldn't hear, so I had to ask him to repeat himself. "Sir, what did you say?"

"Follow your dreams," he said, louder. "Life is too short; never give up on your dreams! And if you don't have any dreams, you'd better start thinking about some."

Dreams… I wondered what the old man was getting to so I asked him what he meant. As he spoke in soft words, he started me on an adventure I could never have imagined and one I would never forget. Dreaming!

Chapter One

"Nineteen seventeen is when I started dreaming," he said. *What could he be talking about?* I thought. Then the words began to flow from his lips like he was reading a book. I sat and listened, and while I listened I realized I began to see his world and his dream. It was as if the old salty dog was a magician and had put me under a spell.

Back in nineteen seventeen, when I was a child, my older brother, Max, and I lived with our parents on a farm. The farm was in New Brunswick, Canada, near Blacks Harbour. We were Irish descendants and in eighteen forty-six my grandfather Robert immigrated to Canada with his parents during Ireland's great potato famine.

There was fear of civil war in the United States and my great-grandfather James didn't want to worry about food shortages caused by war and civil unrest.

After what he and his family experienced in Ireland during the famine, the decision to go to Canada was easy. Besides, James didn't want to put his family in a harmful situation nor have his children forced to fight a war for another country.

My great-grandfather James knew war would be inevitable because it focused on the Negro slaves and their freedom. The Northern states believed all men were created equal and that a man shouldn't be forced to work for no wages, like an animal. The white population in the Southern states, on the other hand, had grown up with Negroes as slaves and farm workers so they did not think there was cause for war. But if the North wanted to fight, the South would protect their property, which included the slaves.

After settling in Canada, James learned that many of the Irishmen who landed in Boston, New York, and Philadelphia's harbors were forced to serve in the Union army to pay for the right to enter the country. Robert, James's oldest son, was fortunate his father decided to go to Canada instead. If not, Robert may have been forced to fight in the Civil War or pay two hundred dollars. Immigrants barely had clothes to bring with them to North America, let alone money.

My great-grandparents were farmers in Ireland. The Irish always had large families so there were plenty of able hands to work the farms. As farmers, they grew potatoes, grains, rye and corn; so naturally, in Canada they continued the tradition.

James sold much of what he grew to the US Government. Many of the crops grown in the United States came from the Southern states, where the weather was nice all year round. The Northern states had short farming seasons and harsh winters similar to Canada. What the Northern states couldn't grow they purchased from Canada so they could feed their citizens and troops. The Southern states had an advantage with their agriculture and food supply, but the Northern states had a better industrial advantage and a monetary support system for their war efforts.

Around eighteen fifty-two, James planted several successful seasons of crops and raised enough money to buy additional land. My great-grandparents were proud people and wanted to pass on what they could to their children.

When my grandfather Robert turned twenty-one, James passed the farm and business on to him. Robert was also very successful at farming. When the Civil War ended, the Reconstruction Period in the United States began. The business relationship James had established during this time with the United States Government, along with the money saved from selling crops, enabled Robert to purchase several more parcels of land during his lifetime.

When my father was old enough to inherit the farms, he really didn't want to continue in the family farming business. He didn't want to work every day of the week and confine his children to the same life. He didn't think farming was a bad business, because his grandfather and father were financially successful, but he wanted more from life.

My father told my mother that he had always wanted to start a distillery. Stories had been told about how his ancestors had distilled alcohol in Ireland. Several recipes were passed down from generation to generation in his family. Father would use the recipes to start his new business.

Before the turn of the century Father told Mother the world was changing, and they needed to change with it. Anyone can farm, but those who were willing to take risks would prosper with the changes time would bring in the new industrial world. Before Max and I were born, my father and mother met with the farmhands. Father offered the workers an opportunity to lease his farms. Each man, or team of men, could farm divisions of his land. All would have support from Father and his farm equipment. Whoever decided to accept Father's offer would be required to farm the land, continue to grow potatoes, grains, corn, and other saleable crops. In addition, Father would purchase all excess crops grown to use for the distillery. This would allow the farmhands the opportunity to pay the farm lease and earn a good living.

Father was a smart man and knew how to make a prosperous living at whatever he did. All along, he had only wanted the best for himself, Mother, and all who worked for him. Living as a farmer was very hard work and required many talents. Equipment needed to be repaired;

silos, barns, storage sheds and anything else that couldn't be bought had to be built. Father learned many trades as a farmer and used his talents to build the distillery.

Although Mother was very reluctant to take the risk, she agreed to help and support Father's idea. Mother feared there would be nothing left of the successful business my great-grandparents and grandparents built for my father to someday pass on to their children. Her dreams were that her children would go to college and become educated. After all, with news coming from the United States of how businesses were becoming successful due to the industrial revolution, she knew educated men would be highly sought after to run the new businesses.

No generation in our family, including my father and mother, had the opportunity to go to college, let alone finish grade school. Mother wanted to break that cycle. She also feared, when she had children, their chances to go to college would disappear with this new venture her husband wanted to pursue.

Father had filed the necessary documents with the Canadian Government so he could start the distillery legally. Since our family had employed many of the local townspeople on the farm and Father was always available to help anyone who asked, there was little local resistance or concern. Most of the locals did think Father was a little crazy for wanting to give up farming; but they also thought that if anyone could do it, he could.

Father built a great business and reputation in Canada and the northeastern United States. Since the turn of the century, Father and Mother sold fine liquors and spirits to the new American "aristocrats," the new millionaires who had built the United States during the Industrial Revolution.

Just as my mother had predicted, these newly rich businessmen built enormous palaces along the coast of New England. From the rocky shores of Maine to the sandy beaches of Rhode Island, beautiful vacation homes and summer palaces were constructed. Father made and sold all the fine liquor and spirits they required to entertain their friends and business associates in grand fashion. My father and mother could not have been happier.

Max, my older brother, was born in December nineteen hundred and six; and I followed a few years after, in July of nineteen hundred and eight. Mother finally had the family she always dreamt of, two sons who would grow up, go to college, and become prosperous businessmen.

On January sixteenth, nineteen twenty, the United States enacted the Eighteenth Amendment to the Constitution and the Volstead Act. This amendment prohibited the manufacture, sale and distribution of liquor in the United States. A majority of our liquor business was in the United States, and Father feared we would lose everything. The farms needed the distillery to maintain the leases, and we needed the liquor sales to the United States to pay our workers and save the money needed for Max and my college education.

In early nineteen nineteen, Father's wealthy customers in the United States knew that Prohibition would soon be enacted and enforced so they bought as much liquor from my father as they could store. Fortunately, the profits from the increased sales helped the distillery and the farms through the early years after Prohibition began. My parents still had liquor sales in Canada, so all was not lost. Father and Mother developed a plan to closely watch their spending and find other uses for their crops.

Since the First World War had already started in Europe, Canada was called upon to support England with as much as it could. There were campaigns in Canada to support the war effort by enlisting in the military or selling surplus materials and crops to Great Britain, just in case the war spread through Europe. Since the United States liquor sales were gone, Father decided to focus on the farms. After all, he had a much larger family to support. Not only did he have two young children to feed, he also hired many of the surrounding townspeople to work on the farms and at the distillery. Without his businesses the region would suffer economically.

In nineteen twenty-two, the roaring twenties were in full swing in the United States. I was fourteen and Max was sixteen. Prohibition had been lingering in the States for the past two years. Mother knew that if Prohibition continued a few more years it would hurt business dramatically. Mother's earlier fears of her children not attending college were beginning to reappear.

Father had also planned for us to go to college and didn't think Prohibition would last very long. In Canada, manufacturing and selling spirits was still legal during the US Prohibition, but there were new laws imposed. The Canadian Government recognized a great financial opportunity with United States Prohibition and added an export tax on all liquor. The new liquor export tax (and our having only Canadian liquor sales), exportation of crops to Great Britain, and the cutbacks my father initiated barely generated enough to pay living expenses, employee wages, and a little something toward our college education fund.

Father made the best Canadian whiskey for miles around. Everyone in the region knew of him and considered him a smart businessman. During the summer of nineteen twenty-two, a man from Boston, known only as Joe, came to Blacks Harbour. Father had sold liquor to Joe previously but had never met him face to face. Joe came to offer my father a lucrative business proposition. He wanted to buy Father's Canadian whiskey and spirits; all we could make. There was one stipulation, though; Father would be required to deliver it to Boston. The money Joe offered was four to five times more than we had been paid in the past.

Around the time Joe came to visit my parents, ninety percent of all liquor sold in the United States had come illegally from Canada. Toronto had become the liquor capital of Canada. In Detroit, Michigan, there was a Jewish mob called the Purple Gang. All liquor transported to and throughout the United States was protected and distributed by these men and their affiliates such as Al Capone in Chicago.

These men were ruthless enforcers, and anyone trying to move liquor into the United States without their consent would be made examples of. The Purple Gang would buy good Canadian liquor and dilute it to double or triple their sales. The only other place to buy large quantities of liquor was in the Kentucky hills, but it was cheap liquor. Moonshiners used sugar instead of corn. The cheap liquor became known as "White Lightning" because of its clear color and harsh taste. Good liquor was very expensive and hard to find in the States.

The common folks in the United States didn't really care what the liquor tasted like when they bought it as long as it was easy to get, cheap, and could get you drunk. Moonshiners had plenty of customers. Our customers were sophisticated and very wealthy and would pay anything to get our straight Canadian whiskey. We didn't want to deal with the Purple Gang because we knew they would dilute our liquor, put in additives to darken it up, and leave our labels on the bottles to get more money.

Father and Mother spent much time thinking about Joe's proposition, but in the end decided against it. They feared being caught by the US Government and going to prison. Prison meant the Canadian Government would confiscate our home and business. If caught, my parents would lose everything they built. Also, if the Purple Gang or anyone affiliated with them learned of our deal with Joe, not only would our business be at risk but our lives, too.

By this time I was a sophomore in high school, and Max was a senior. We both had visions of college life, girls, living in a big city, and learning business and engineering to help with our parents' businesses when we returned home. Everyone in town knew Max and I would take over the businesses after college. For now, playing baseball behind the distillery with friends from school was all I cared about. I knew in a few years we would be off to college, so I enjoyed the free time.

Chapter Two

Growing up on the southeastern shore of New Brunswick was wonderful. The air was always crisp and cool and you could run for miles without ever breaking a sweat. Father didn't mind me not working on the farms or in the distillery because he wanted me to enjoy childhood before I went off to college. He didn't get to stay in school very long because his parents needed his help with their growing farm business. As long as I completed my schoolwork, received good grades, and finished my chores on time, he was happy.

On a beautiful late summer day in nineteen twenty-four, Max and I were in the field behind our barn completing our chores and enjoying the nice weather when we heard a loud noise coming toward us from overhead. The sound was unrecognizable. It was so remote and peaceful where we lived that you could hear the birds flutter their wings when they flew off the top of the barn. We had no idea what was making the noise or why the noise was coming from the sky.

Through a break in the clouds we could finally see what it was. "Look," I said to Max, "it's an airplane." We had read about airplanes in newspapers and had seen pictures of them in magazines but had never actually seen a real one. As the sound became louder and the airplane flew closer, we realized it was having problems. I had envisioned airplanes flying as smoothly as a bird, but this airplane seemed to have serious trouble.

We ran from behind the barn to a field beyond the woods to get a better look without the obstruction of trees. Max ran ahead of me and looked back once in a while to see if I was keeping up. As we ran through the trees and approached the field, the noise grew louder and louder. We thought the airplane was going to try to land in the field. Just then, the plane flew directly overhead with a loud roar. It seemed to be only a few hundred feet above us. The roar of the engine was deafening as it choked for fuel to continue running.

The airplane circled back over us once again. Just as we arrived at the field, the airplane had banked one last time to straighten out so it could land. Max and I watched in amazement as the men flying the airplane tried to keep it stable so they could clear the trees and land safely. Although the airplane had engine trouble, it was barely supporting itself enough to maneuver and glide.

Keeping the airplane from spinning out of control when it hit the ground looked almost impossible. The field was wet and the mud was thick with brush and tree stumps, but the men had no choice, they needed to land soon.

We could see the faces of the men as they approached. To our horror the enormous airplane landed on its pontoons and slid in the muddy field. The wooden propeller on the engine shattered into splinters as the nose of the airplane tipped forward. Suddenly, the airplane's wing hit a tree and spun around, flipping violently forward on to its back. Our fear and thoughts of death took over all our senses. We could only watch helplessly.

When the airplane finally came to a complete stop, Max and I ran over to see if anyone was still alive. Smoke was still coming from the engine, and we could smell fuel. Growing up around the distillery, we knew how flammable the fuel vapors could be and how the tiniest spark could ignite. We tried to be careful because we knew our clothes rubbing against the tall weeds could create a spark. The tiniest spark would cause us, the airplane, and any survivors to blow up.

As we approached the airplane, we could hear moans and cries for help. After seeing the way the airplane crashed with parts scattered throughout the field, we couldn't believe the men flying it were still alive.

God was definitely watching over the men that day. I was able to get to the front of the airplane and could see where the fuel was coming from. The men flying the airplane were strapped into their seats by some kind of belt and were hanging upside down. I pulled the brush and debris away to look further under the airplane. Both men were slightly bleeding from their heads and were semi-conscious.

Max had somehow managed to get into the airplane through a hole created by the crash landing. Max checked to see if anyone was seriously hurt, but both men seemed to be all right. As Max loosened the belts to free the men, I continued to remove the brush. Finally, Max was able to slide each man down to me below the airplane. I slid them forward to get them as far from the airplane as possible for fear it still may explode. Once away and free from harm we removed our shirts and placed whatever cloth we could find over the wounds to slow their bleeding.

By this time, Mother and some employees from the distillery had reached the field and helped to nurse the men. Unbelievably, both men were not badly injured, only confused and in shock from the violent landing, with little loss of blood. We took them to our home for further care while the farmhands put out the smoldering wreck.

As the news of the crash spread locally of how Max and I had pulled the men from the battered wreck, people started calling us heroes. We didn't consider ourselves heroes. We only did what our parents always taught us; help anyone in need.

Later we learned the men who flew the airplane were called pilots. One of the pilots was an officer and the other was an enlisted man in the US Army Aviation Service. The airplane was part of a four-airplane team attempting to be the first to complete an around-the-world flight beginning in Seattle, Washington. They were finishing the last 2,200 miles back to Seattle when the crash occurred. We also learned this was not the only plane that had crashed during the trip.

Of the four Douglas World Cruisers, or DWC's as they were referred to, the *Seattle*, the *Boston*, the *Chicago* and the *New Orleans*, which left Seattle on April fourth, nineteen twenty-four, only the *New Orleans* and *Chicago* completed the trip. Soon after departing Washington State, the *Seattle* had been lost over Dutch Harbour, Alaska, during a Pacific storm, and during the final stage of the journey, the *Boston* was the crash Max and I witnessed near our home.

Members of the US Army Aviation Service and the Douglas Aircraft Company came to Blacks Harbour to retrieve the pilots and survey the damaged *Boston DWC*.

It was determined that the fuel pump malfunctioned and starved the engine, which caused the airplane to lose power and stall. Because of the long flight over the Atlantic Ocean, moisture may have also contaminated the fuel.

The airplane wreckage was too badly damaged and stuck into the muddy forest to remove it. Besides, getting heavy equipment into that part of the forest for the removal would be too expensive. The Douglas Aircraft Company decided to repay us for our help; and since the airplane was on our property, we were awarded the rights to salvage. All the surrounding townspeople were forced to sign documents agreeing we would not tell anyone of the airplane's location. This had been done to keep scavengers from coming onto our land and to keep competing airplane manufacturers from finding the *Boston*. The local newspaper reports said the *Boston* was lost in the mid-Atlantic.

Father found some use for what remained of the metal skin and fuselage. He used whatever parts he could remove from the airplane at the distillery and the farm. The engine was too large to use on the farm or the distillery, so Max and I removed it with our tractor from the remaining carcass and brought it back to our farm. Max only helped me remove the engine because he thought if the business really needed money we could sell it.

I loved to tinker with machines or whatever I could get my hands on. Max was more studious and always gave me a hard time for spending hours trying to invent new things. I had my father's ingenuity and he had Mother's smarts. Max thought our time was best spent figuring out how to improve the business, not "playing with machines," as he called it.

In my spare time, I built a frame to hold the airplane engine so I could repair it. With tools from the businesses, Gus and I would spend hours marveling over this beautiful airplane engine. Gus was the son of one of Father's employees. We tried to understand how it worked, but after weeks of looking and tinkering, Mother suggested I write the Douglas Aircraft Company for some help.

John Holland, the engineer from Douglas Aircraft who had inspected the crash, wrote back to tell us the Liberty engine's fuel filter and pump were most likely the problem. He said he wasn't sure if there were any internal parts damaged from the propeller snapping off but if not, the fuel parts could be replaced easily.

In preparation for the around-the-world flight, Douglas Aircraft had sent airplane and engine parts to destinations along the flight path to assist with repairs if needed. Douglas Aircraft needed to ensure a successful circumnavigation of the world to have any chance of a military contract with the United States Government. As luck would have it, Mr. Holland said that parts for the engine repair could be found in Toronto and could be shipped to us. He reminded me of our consent not to disclose the location of the airplane and would make arrangements to ship us the parts.

About six weeks later, we received the new fuel pump and filter with a letter from Mr. Holland instructing me how to install and prime the unit. Gus, having more experience with pumps and gasoline-powered engines while working at the farm and distillery, showed me what to do.

With the new fuel pump and filter installed, and the Liberty engine securely mounted to the frame Gus and I built, we prepared to start the engine. The engine, when mounted in the airplane, was started by rotating the propeller. Since the propeller had been broken off during the crash, Gus and I attached a pulley to the propeller shaft. With a leather drive belt, taken from one of Father's farm machines, we connected it to the Liberty engine's propeller shaft and the drive shaft of the tractor.

After several attempts to start the Liberty with no success, we asked Max for help. Max wanted nothing to do with our engine since it was of no use to the business.

I wrote to Mr. Holland again and although he and the Douglas Aircraft Company were grateful to us for helping the pilots, he didn't have any more time to assist us. Mr. Holland and Douglas Aircraft were preparing contracts with the United States Government in addition to redesigning the airplane and engine based on information learned from the around-the-world flight. The *Boston* pilots we had helped were also preparing to fly a new *Boston II* built with the changes, and once again fly around the world. Gus and I decided to cover the Liberty engine in the shed for storage and come back to it when more time, information, and help was available.

Chapter Three

During dinner one evening I listened as Father and Max discussed the condition of the business. With Prohibition still in full force, it was getting tougher and tougher to meet financial obligations. Max and Father had done all they could to make the business more efficient and minimize spending, but it was still tough making ends meet.

With knowledge Max gained from helping run the distillery, Father decided it was time for him to attend Harvard in Boston. I wanted to attend the Massachusetts Institute of Technology in Cambridge and had to convince Father to let me go.

Harvard provided the courses Max needed to learn more about business, and MIT would allow me to study chemical and mechanical engineering. Enough money had been saved through the years for our college education, and Mother wanted it to go to use before Father changed his mind. Mother worried Father would use the money to help the business survive the Prohibition era.

Max and I had both achieved good grades in high school and had received excellent recommendations from our schools and local businessmen. We were not sure if the grades and recommendations would help since we lived in a remote area in Canada and virtually no one in the United States had heard of Blacks Harbour. Mother became very excited when she learned Father had agreed to let Max and me attend college.

During the summer of nineteen twenty-six, Max and I traveled to Boston to enroll in school and to take our entrance exams. We departed Blacks Harbour by ferry to Bath, Maine, and then traveled by train for the final route to Boston. Mother had seen us off on our journey and wished us good fortune during our travels. Max and I had never traveled far from home before and for us to go away for such a long time made Mother sad. Although she didn't say anything, you could see the sadness in her face as the ferry departed.

Once in Boston, we found a room to rent until we could get situated. With a good basic high school education and Max's experience running Father's businesses and maintaining the financial ledgers, Max passed his entrance exams with little difficulty and was accepted into Harvard. I was very proud of Max, because he had worked so hard to prepare for the exams.

My experience in building equipment on the farm and distillery, however, didn't really help with my admission into MIT. The exam required me to demonstrate math, calculus, and physics skills. Since I had very little knowledge in these areas, I was told to seek enrollment in another "less demanding" school or get tutored and re-enroll when I felt capable.

After informing Max of my dilemma with MIT, he realized how disappointed I was. Max decided to help me with the math I needed to learn so I could take the enrollment test again at a future date. Max also wanted me to go to college because he knew I would be needed to help with the businesses when we returned home.

My stay in Boston began as a difficult one. Since I had not been accepted to school, I had no place to live. Max had to rent an apartment off campus so we could live together. The money saved for my education would be used for the rent until I could find work. Max preferred living at school, so he wouldn't be disturbed while studying, but reluctantly agreed to help me.

Boston was a bustling city in the mid-nineteen twenties. The city was full of life, prosperity, and opportunity. I lived in an isolated area of Canada all my life, and being in Boston was overwhelming. Although my first impression of Boston was the rejection I faced at MIT and the depression I felt from not being able to attend college, I realized that, in the United States, you could do anything and be whatever you wanted. It was up to you to make your own future prosperous.

While growing up in Canada, I was fortunate in that my parents owned their own businesses. I soon realized how little material possessions many of my friends had back in Blacks Harbour and the surrounding towns. I never really understood the different classes, poor, middle class, or rich. To me, there were only two classes: either you were very rich or you weren't. I gained great respect for the men who worked for my father. Father paid well but his men had little work to choose from. They needed to feed and clothe their families so most took whatever work was available.

I also understood the sacrifices my father and mother made for Max and me so we could get a higher education. They sacrificed their lives for us. They could have used the college money saved to help with the family businesses, or have taken nice trips to see the world. Instead, they stuck to their plan and goals so Max and I could have better lives and our children could have brighter futures.

I had never experienced so much in such a short time. People, horses, trolleys, motorcycles, bicycles, and automobiles all shared the roads. In Blacks Harbour, you would only see an automobile every once in a while. Only the very rich owned automobiles for pleasure and they were usually businessmen and vacationers from the United States passing through on their way to Saint John. Here in Boston it seemed everyone owned an automobile or some type of powered transportation.

Watching people bustling around Boston was exciting. Looking up at all the buildings and walking through the crowded streets made me feel very small and unimportant. In Blacks Harbour, I was the son of a successful businessman and was treated with respect. In Boston, I was just another person in a crowded city. No one knew who I was or where I came from. A man could get lost in the sea of people in Boston and no one would even notice, or care.

As I walked the streets of Boston looking for work, I began to see the commercial side of the city. There were beautiful, tall ships in the harbor offloading goods coming from far-off countries across the oceans and loading products to ship back. Boston, at the time, was one of the more important ports for international trade and worldwide travel. There were open markets on the docks and streets, with merchants selling everything from fresh fruits and vegetables to slaughtered cows and hogs, ivory carvings from Africa, and trinkets from Asia and South America. You could buy anything you wanted in Boston, all you needed was money or something of value to trade.

There was also another side to the city I began to see. In the back streets and alleys there were many homeless children. These children, who could not have been any older than nine or ten, and some as young as seven or eight, worked in the factories. They were only children. They should have been in school or with their parents being cared for. Where were their parents? How could they have been left alone in this big city to fend for themselves? They needed to be loved like Max and I were when we were growing up. They needed to be children, to have fun, playing in fields and laughing.

I couldn't imagine growing up like these children. I wondered where they would sleep at night or where they would get their next meal. Many begged, stole, or rummaged through trash to get by. These children banded together to form gangs so they could protect themselves. After all, they had no one else. I often wondered how they got here. Why was this happening? Didn't they have relatives or someone who would let them live with them? This was the United States and Boston was a great city with lots of life and prosperity. Seeing all this taught me a valuable lesson. Even in times of prosperity there are still dark and hidden sides to society.

Being out of work and living off my college fund wasn't a comfortable feeling. If I continued to be out of work, I would deplete the money my parents had saved and would never make it to college. I had to find work soon and start paying my way or else Max wouldn't think twice about putting me on a train or boat back to Blacks Harbour. I was surprised he hadn't already.

Max would have preferred if I weren't there. After all, I was only in the way of his education. It would be better if he didn't have to worry about me. Max hadn't said it but I knew he needed to focus on school and not wonder what I was doing roaming the streets of Boston alone.

Living with Max was not that bad for me. As we grew up, although Max was just a few years older than I, we didn't spend lots of time together. I had my friends and Max had his. When we were younger, I would have preferred sneaking around with Max and the older boys. We were somewhat opposites. I liked building things out of anything I could find, and Max liked reading and studying. He spent most of his free time at the library.

While sharing the apartment in Boston, there were many evenings Max and I would talk during and after dinner. We were both a little homesick and our company was all we had to keep us feeling close to Blacks Harbour. Max felt an obligation to make sure I found work and that I continued to study to prepare for enrolling into MIT. I began to see how mature Max was for his age and began to understand how immature I was for my age.

I started to grow closer to Max, and rely on him more. I thought that would never happen. Max was trying to teach me to be responsible for myself and to our family. I slowly learned to be responsible and to think about helping our parents' businesses grow when I returned home. Max and I both knew we would inherit the businesses, but at that time finding work became my top priority.

As I searched for work, I met many interesting people. There were the factory owners and supervisors who wanted nothing from workers but long hours for little pay. Women and children got the hard and menial jobs because no one else would work under the conditions they were exposed to.

Coming from Canada, I was certainly at a disadvantage. I admit I was naïve about city life and the many jobs available. Restaurants, hotels, charter boats, rail lines, buses, and transportation companies all had their underground hiring methods. You needed to know someone in those businesses in order to get a job. It became very frustrating for me. Every time I applied for work I was asked, "Who sent you to us?" Knowing no one in Boston or the United States, I had no answer and was turned down for job after job.

During my search, I noticed a gasoline filling station in town that was always busy. Although there were many gasoline stations in Boston, this particular one had more customers than all the rest. The owner seemed to be overwhelmed with work every time I passed by. I decided I would ask him if he would hire me. I planned to stop in during his busy time so few questions would be asked of me.

With customers yelling for gasoline, water for overheated engines, and numerous repairs, I ran over and just started helping his customers. The owner of the gasoline filling station looked at me in a curious way as I assisted his customers with simple tasks, then watched as I collected money and tips for the services.

Without speaking a word to the owner, I worked at a distance from him all that afternoon and into the evening hours. He could tell I was not one of the homeless boys or a con man because of my courteous responses to some of the more irate customers.

As evening grew closer, I finished helping the last few customers and approached the owner. I gave him all the money I collected, including the tips. After all, we had no working agreement. The owner of the gasoline filling station complimented me for being so polite to all the customers and said I could keep the tips I earned. He asked me my name and where I came from. I told him who I was and that I just arrived from Canada. I also explained my situation with MIT and that I needed to work until I could get accepted into college. He agreed to let me continue to work the rest of the week only for tips. He also said, "If you continue to be polite and show up for work on time each day, I will consider letting you stay on as long as I need you."

We agreed that I would start at seven each morning and work until closing, at nine o'clock in the evening. I was allowed two breaks during the day and time off for lunch. I couldn't thank him enough for his generosity. With that agreement, he told me his name was Albert Hoffman and shook my hand. I finally found work and couldn't wait to get back to the apartment to tell Max.

Later that evening, when Max arrived home, I had already made dinner for him and me. I could see Max was tired from studying and going to classes all day so I decided to let him know of my good fortune after we finished dinner. It was difficult to hold in the excitement of finding work. All I could think about was how proud Max would be of me and happy that we didn't have to use my college fund for the rent.

After dinner I showed Max the tips I had earned. He asked where the money had come from. I explained all about my day at the gasoline filling station and that I was asked to return for the remainder of the week as a trial period. He could see how excited I was and said that I made him proud. He also said he would wake me in the morning so I wouldn't be late for work.

I was still too excited to go to sleep that evening so I decided to write a letter to my parents to let them know how Max and I were doing. While writing the first few lines I couldn't keep my eyes open. My exhaustion had overcome my excitement and soon I fell asleep.

The next morning Max woke me up as promised. I was still tired but jumped out of bed so I could start my first full day of work in Boston. It was a beautiful day, the sun was shining and there wasn't a cloud in the sky. I made some lunch from the leftover dinner the evening before, thanked Max for waking me up, and set out for the gasoline filling station.

I planned to arrive at six thirty the first morning to show Mr. Hoffman that I really wanted the work. Although I arrived early, there was already a line of customers waiting for gasoline. The local deliverymen needed to fill up their trucks so they didn't have to stop during the day. I got right to work, and we finished the last truck around eight that morning. There was finally a short idle period of about ten or fifteen minutes. Mr. Hoffman told me it was time for the morning break so we went inside for coffee.

While having coffee, Mr. Hoffman wanted to learn a little bit more about me. I told him I was from Blacks Harbour, New Brunswick, Canada, and that my parents owned farms and a distillery. I also told him I had a brother named Max who was attending Harvard and that we shared an apartment until I could get into MIT. I explained the situation about the distillery and Prohibition and how Max and I were expected to take over the businesses after we graduated from college. Mr. Hoffman interrupted me and said we would continue the conversation later. Customers were at the pumps and we needed to get back to work.

During the remainder of the day we didn't have time to stop. Customers continued to come in all day for fuel and minor repairs. We were only able to eat our lunch when time permitted. The first day of work flew by. Keeping busy all day was exciting. I earned more tips and again thanked Mr. Hoffman for hiring me. Just before we closed up the shop he told me, "From now on you can call me Albert." After that I told him I would see him in the morning and walked home exhausted.

I continued to arrive early at work each day for the remainder of my trial week. The fast pace never ended, but all the tips I earned made up for all the hard work. Since it was now Saturday, and my trial week was over, I was curious to find out if Albert would let me stay on.

Saturday was slower than weekdays so I knew we would have some time to talk. Early that Saturday afternoon Albert asked me to wait for him in the office while he helped serve a customer. When he came back in he asked me, in his deep German accent, to sit down. I thought, because of the way he asked, that I would not be able to continue to work. To my surprise, Albert said he was very pleased with the way I helped customers and arrived early each morning. He told me he would pay me twenty cents each day and I could keep all tips.

Albert said there would be a few conditions. I would be required to arrive on time, not miss days unless it was absolutely necessary, and he made me promise I would continue to study in order to reapply for college.

Albert went on to say he had been fortunate to have studied engineering at a university in Germany. After he graduated from the university, he was employed by Daimler to be an apprentice to the automobile craftsmen. He told me that at Daimler automobiles were handcrafted one at a time by a team of skilled engineers. He had the opportunity to learn all aspects of automobile design, manufacture, and assembly by some of the best craftsmen in the world. He was not paid much money but the experience he gained would allow him to own and operate his own business someday.

Albert was a very intellectual and disciplined man, well educated, and with many years of experience. He was tall and lean and had the appearance of a confident man. He had not married and had no family in the United States. He preferred to be alone because he had seen many displaced families during the First World War in Europe. He didn't want to raise children in such a turbulent world and felt a wife would not allow him to move or travel whenever he wanted.

While living in Germany and working at Daimler, Albert had heard of a man named Ransom E. Olds who was building automobiles in the United States. Olds had developed a way to manufacture automobiles continuously on an assembly line and Albert was curious to see it for himself. In nineteen hundred and nine at Daimler, based on the way they assembled in a team, it required one thousand and seven hundred workers to build one thousand automobiles a year. In nineteen hundred and four the Olds factory, with the assembly line technique, produced over five thousand five hundred automobiles in a single year with far fewer workers.

The Olds workers didn't need to be skilled in all aspects of automobile manufacturing, they only needed to know how to work with simple hand tools to assemble individual components and install them. This allowed Olds to pay lower wages, because the workers were considered much less skilled than the craftsmen.

After Germany lost the First World War to Great Britain, Albert decided to leave his homeland and come to the United States.

Germans were a deliberate and determined race. He knew it was a matter of time before Germany would again enter into war.

When Albert reached Michigan, he learned that Henry Ford perfected the assembly line production plant and was manufacturing more automobiles than any other company in the world. In nineteen hundred and twenty, Ford sold half the automobiles purchased in the United States.

Albert managed to find work at Ford's plant in Highland Park, Michigan. Because Albert was formally educated in automobile engineering and had experience with turbocharged and supercharged gasoline-powered engines, the Ford Motor Company hired him because they wanted to learn more about German quality, engineering, and manufacturing techniques. Ford also knew, in order to develop more horsepower, speed, and economy, he would need to develop and integrate its own turbocharger or supercharger.

Albert understood Ford's motives and really didn't care what Ford thought of him. Albert had his own motives. He just wanted a job so he could remain in the United States and not have to return to Germany. Albert's goal was to live in the United States and start his own business. At first, he thought about designing and building his own automobiles, but later he realized there was too much competition in the United States.

Albert decided that with all the automobiles being manufactured using the assembly line process, the vast majority of the public could afford them but quality was compromised. In addition, roads were nonexistent outside the larger cities and automobiles would be battered when driven on rural dirt roads or cross country. This meant many repairs would be needed and lots of gasoline would need to be purchased.

While Albert worked at Ford he saved enough money to start the business he wanted. Through the contacts he made at Ford, he learned how to purchase replacement parts directly from manufacturers who supported Ford, Olds, and the other automobile manufacturers.

It was obvious to me that Albert made the correct decision.

Everyone in Boston knew of Albert's talent to repair any automobile quickly. The local trucking and delivery businesses couldn't survive without him. They relied on his abilities.

Albert taught me everything he knew about gasoline and diesel-powered engines. In addition, he taught me mathematics and physics to help with my re-enrollment into MIT. Although Albert spoke with a heavy German accent, we understood each other very well. It seemed Albert was gifted with a talent to know what people were thinking before the words could be spoken. After a while, I could tell what he was thinking also. We made a great team. I got the feeling Albert thought of me, not so much as an employee, but as the son he never had. He also had compassion for me since I, too, was an immigrant.

While working for Albert, the excitement of learning from him and the fast pace of work made the days turn into weeks and the weeks turn into months.

Chapter Four

One afternoon, while Albert was out picking up parts, a man in a beautiful black automobile drove into the filling station. I walked outside to see the beautiful machine and wondered who owned it. As I approached the automobile, the owner looked at me in a peculiar way. I recognized him but I couldn't remember where I knew him from.

I told the man that Albert was out and would return soon. He said he had spoken to Albert the evening before and would leave the Packard for service. I opened the garage door so the driver could pull in. The owner gave me the key and said he would wait for Albert to contact him. Another automobile followed the men to the filling station. The driver and owner of the Packard got into the waiting automobile, then drove away.

A short while later Albert returned. I told him about the automobile in the garage, pointed to the key on the rack, and went back to work. Albert asked me to unload the parts from the truck and to bring them into the garage. The parts he had gone to purchase were for the black Packard left in the garage. Albert spent the remainder of the day and the entire evening servicing the Packard. Just after nine that evening, I closed up the filling station and left for home. Albert was still working in the garage.

The following morning, I arrived earlier than usual. I found Albert asleep at the desk in the office. I woke him up when I walked in and asked him why he was still here. He said he stayed the entire evening to finish the work on the Packard. He said it needed to be completed this morning because the owner wanted it delivered by seven a.m. Albert asked me to pull the Packard out of the garage and he went into the lavatory to wash up.

A chill ran up my spine when Albert asked me to pull the beautiful automobile out of the garage. I thought about the Packard all evening and imagined myself driving it through town as if I were a rich man. I had never been so excited in my life. I couldn't wait to drive it. When I started it up, it purred like a kitten. I stepped on the accelerator and could feel the powerful engine come to life. Albert sure had a knack for tuning engines. As I pulled the Packard up in front of the filling station, Albert walked out and told me to follow him in the truck.

I pulled the truck up behind Albert and as we set out from the North End, everyone watched as we passed with the beautiful black Packard. We traveled to the East Side and stopped in front of a bank. I thought, *Only a banker could own such a beautiful and expensive machine.* Albert parked the Packard, walked over to the truck, and handed me a dollar. He told me to buy myself coffee and breakfast in the restaurant across the street and wait there for him. I backed the truck into an alley and went to the restaurant as directed.

I had not eaten in a restaurant since I had left Blacks Harbour. To save money, Max and I bought groceries and cooked our meals at the apartment. When I was younger, we would only eat at a restaurant to celebrate birthdays. Mother thought birthdays were a special occasion and should be celebrated. Father, on the other hand, always felt uncomfortable in restaurants. Most of his business deals were arranged in restaurants by his customers. To him, being in a restaurant was usually not a pleasurable experience because he had to discuss business. He never really got to enjoy being served his meal while at business dinners.

I walked into the restaurant and found an open stool at the counter. From where I sat I could see the bank across the street and would watch to see when Albert was ready to leave. In the city, the restaurant tables were reserved for wealthy families or businessmen and their companions. White workers, like Albert and I, were required to eat at the counter and colored people were required to eat outside.

That morning I had left the apartment early to get to the filling station, so I had had no breakfast. The aroma of fried bacon and eggs in addition to the percolating coffee smelled wonderful. My mouth watered as I imagined what I would order. It was very busy in the restaurant, and the waitresses passed me by several times. Without looking at me, one waitress stopped for a moment, poured me a cup of coffee, placed silverware in front of me, and dashed off to deliver someone's breakfast. I didn't mind the wait. It gave me a few moments to relax. I knew once Albert returned we would leave and go straight back to work.

Finally, one of the waitresses stopped and asked me if I had decided what I wanted. I looked up at her and nearly fell off my stool. As I stared with a look of amazement on my face she asked me again, "Are you ready to order?" She was stunningly beautiful. I still could not get words out. As she stepped away, with a smile, she said, "I'll be back in a minute to take your order." I guess she knew I was attracted to her.

I picked up a menu and pretended I was deciding what to have. I peered over the top of the menu to watch her as she served other customers. I had never seen such a beautiful woman. In Blacks Harbour, I knew many girls, but none that captured my attention as she did. Her name, Shannon, was embroidered on her blouse. She had long, curly, light strawberry-blond-colored hair. Her skin was milky white and she had features that resembled an angel. At that time, Shannon was a common name. Like most Irish girls, she was probably named after a grandmother or great-grandmother.

Shannon soon came back for my order. In addition to the coffee, I ordered a short stack of pancakes and bacon. I didn't have much time to eat because I knew Albert would be back soon. We left the garage unattended and locked up. Just as my breakfast was served, I could see Albert walking out of the bank building. He came into the restaurant and sat next to me. Apparently, Albert frequented the restaurant because Shannon asked if he wanted his usual order and whether she should wrap it so he could take it with him. Albert nodded yes and waited with me for his order.

As I ate my pancakes, Albert said he would be taking the truck and driving back alone. I couldn't understand why but he said the man at the bank who owned the Packard asked if he needed his driver to return him to the station. Albert said I had been waiting in the restaurant to bring him back. The banker told Albert he recognized me when he dropped the Packard at the gasoline filling station and wanted me to wait at the restaurant for him.

A few minutes later, Albert was given his wrapped breakfast and told me to pay the bill when I was done. I handed Albert the keys to the truck and he walked away. As instructed, I stayed to finish. While I ate, the banker walked over from across the street. When he walked into the restaurant, everyone either said hello or waved to him. I presumed since he worked across the street, everyone knew him. As the banker walked through the restaurant, he stopped to talk to some men in the far corner. He whispered to one of the men, turned back to me, and motioned with his hand for me to follow him.

The banker walked down a corridor toward the lavatories and passed through an unmarked door. I quickly finished my meal, wiped the crumbs from my face, and raised my hand to get Shannon's attention. Shannon walked over and said the meals were already paid for and I shouldn't keep the banker waiting. I put the dollar back in my pocket and left five cents as a tip. As I stood up I brushed the crumbs from the front of my shirt and followed in the banker's path.

At the end of the corridor, I opened the door and walked in. There was a desk in front of me with two chairs. The banker stood behind the desk and the man to whom he whispered walked in behind me. The man moved a carpet aside in front of the desk and lifted a hatch in the floor. I thought it was a delivery entrance. I followed the two men down the steps and entered a large room that resembled the restaurant upstairs. The room was brightly lit, with a large mahogany counter. Tables were set up around the room and a simple stage was up against a long brick wall. Behind the counter were glass shelves and mirrors.

The banker motioned for me to sit at a table and asked me if I wanted anything. Since I had just finished breakfast, I said, "No, thank you." As I looked at the banker closer, I finally recognized him. He was the man from Boston who had visited our distillery four years earlier. I stood up and said, "You're Joe, aren't you?"

At first he looked at the other man, then turned back to me. He didn't respond to my question directly but politely said, "You have a good memory kid; you were only a boy the last time I saw you. Do you know why I asked you here?"

After looking around the room, I realized I was in a speakeasy, or a blind pig as some people called it.

I had read about these places in the newspaper. There were always pictures in the newspapers showing Prohibition law enforcers busting up wooden kegs and bottles filled with liquor. Usually, these places were found and put out of business. I now understood why we had to enter the room through the hatch door and why it was concealed.

Joe and the other man asked me several questions about my parents and their business. They wanted to know if the business was doing well and how I knew Albert. I explained how Max and I came to Boston to attend school but only Max was accepted. I told them it was only by chance that I met Albert. I had been working for Albert for a few months and had been studying to enroll at MIT.

Joe said he knew Albert very well and for that matter knew everyone in Boston. He said he could easily get me enrolled into MIT; but if I were as enterprising as my father, there was plenty of money to be made in Boston without attending school. He talked about how he owned lots of businesses, real estate, and even the restaurant we were in. In addition, he had gained control of the bank across the street when he was only twenty-five. I couldn't help but admire this man and his great business sense and wealth.

We talked for a few more moments and then he stood up to leave. It was almost nine o'clock and the bank would be opening shortly. I said that I needed to get back to the garage soon or I could lose my job. He told me not to worry about my job, that Albert would not fire me. He told the other man to wait a few minutes after he left, lock up the basement, and then drive me back to the gasoline filling station. Just as he started to leave, Joe turned back to me and said we would talk again soon and not to mention to anyone that we had met or what we discussed.

The driver and I waited a minute or two and then climbed back up the stairs through a hatch door. The driver told me his name was Kieran as we drove back to the gasoline filling station. When we arrived, he also reminded me not to forget what Joe had told me, "Don't tell anyone we had met and what we discussed." When I got out of the automobile, I said I wouldn't say anything and walked over to help Albert serve customers.

After my meeting with Joe and Kieran, I wondered why they asked so many questions about my father's business. A few days later, Albert approached me to ask if I needed to talk to someone. I explained to Albert that I had been instructed not to say anything about the meeting at the restaurant. After that I tried to change the subject but Albert knew I was avoiding his questions. Albert told me he would not repeat our conversation or mention anything to anyone. Although he said that, I was still reluctant to repeat what Joe and Kieran had discussed with me. Albert told me I didn't need to explain anything and that he understood.

The next day, Albert approached me again. He said he was still concerned because I was not myself since I had the meeting. Again, he asked me if there was anything he could help me with. I told him it was not the meeting that was distracting me but the thoughts of the waitress in my head. I explained that since I met Shannon at the restaurant, I had a difficult time keeping my mind on anything but her. He looked at me, shrugged and said, "I don't think I can help you with that problem."

I didn't think a woman would have such an effect on me. I usually had a level head and could manage my emotions. Thinking about Shannon, night and day, started to become a problem. My mind would wander with thoughts of *Does she like me? Is she thinking of me as I think of her? Does she even remember me?* Besides, what would she want with a common worker like me? With her beauty she could be with any man she wanted.

I needed to get back to focusing on why I was in Boston. I needed to keep my mind on my work and my studies so I could get back to the real reason I left my family in Canada. I needed to enroll at MIT. I didn't travel all this way and work so hard to be distracted by a woman. Although, having someone to share some time with other than Albert and Max sounded like a welcome treat. Someone to talk to, someone who knew the city and could show me around, someone to share my dreams with, and someone who could help me get through the lonely days when I didn't have work or needed to study.

After I told Albert about Shannon and her effect on me, I don't think he believed she was the only thing on my mind. A few days later, while Albert and I were having our morning break, he said to me, "I started to think about our conversation the other day. Since you said the meeting with Joe wasn't a problem, I thought I would share something with you.

"When I first came to Boston, like you, I didn't know anyone here and had a difficult time finding work. Since I knew no one and I spoke with a heavy German accent, no one would hire me.

"A few days after I arrived, I was walking into town and an automobile passed me. A mile or so up the road it pulled off to the shoulder. The automobile broke down and the driver was trying to get it started. I approached the driver and asked if I could help. The driver looked into the backseat, where a clean-cut gentleman reading a newspaper nodded as though to give his permission. I looked around and noticed a wire had come loose on the ignition, so I reconnected it and signaled him to start the engine. The automobile started right up.

"The driver turned around to speak to the man in the back, and a few moments later the driver approached me while I was waiting on the side of the road. He thanked me for the help and handed me a five dollar bill. I thanked him and said, 'I am new in Boston and can't find work. I'm not a vagrant and I do have skills. Do you know of anyone who might want to hire me?'

"The driver walked back to the passenger and they spoke for a while. When the driver returned he had a telephone number written on a piece of paper. Along with the number was the name of a man. He told me to keep the money and call the number the next afternoon. The name written with the number was 'Joe.'

"The following day I called the number and a secretary asked me to come into the city and wait at a restaurant. The same restaurant where you met Shannon," Albert said. "The reason why I'm telling you this is because Joe was the man who was stranded in the automobile and the same man who met with me at the restaurant. He explained to me, since I had helped him and didn't do it because I knew him, I was genuinely helping a stranger. For this act of kindness he would repay the favor.

"Joe asked me what type of work I was looking for. I thought for a few seconds and said, "I came to Boston to find work but I would prefer owning my own business." We talked for about a half hour more while I explained my background. Joe said he would see what he could do and get back to me. Since I had no telephone where I was staying, he told me to call him in a few days.

"When I returned the call, I was given an address and was told to meet him there in two hours. When I arrived at the address, the building was boarded up with a *For Sale* sign in front. It was an abandoned gasoline filling station, the one we're in. A loan officer from the bank met with me here and said the previous owner had defaulted on a loan and the bank repossessed the property.

"Joe told the loan officer to offer me the business and if I agreed, we would be partners, fifty-fifty. All I needed to do was operate the business and come up with seven hundred dollars to take possession of my half. The contract was already drawn up for me to sign and if I didn't have the money, a loan would be arranged. I agreed, signed the contract, and provided half the payment needed the loan officer asked for. The balance, three hundred and fifty dollars, would be paid back with interest over time from the profits. I actually had all the money he asked for but I knew I would need some money to set up the place and buy supplies.

"When I arrived at the property the next day, several trucks were parked out front. I asked what they needed and was told my partner had arranged for them to help me get the business started. The men unloaded their trucks, opened up the windows, cleaned the garage and office, brought in furniture and tools, and placed a sign out front stating, *Open for Business, Under New Management.* The same afternoon a gasoline tank truck made a delivery and set up the pumps. All I had to do was sign more papers.

"After that day, as you know, delivery trucks arrive each morning and business is constant. The delivery trucks are not all for legitimate business. There are arrangements with several men in town who only purchase gasoline from me, no questions asked. Once or twice a week crates are delivered to the back of the station and a few days later, out-of-town trucks come in to pick them up. I didn't know what was being transferred, and I didn't ask. The reason why I tell you this is because, working with Joe, you will make lots of money but there will be times when you are asked, or told, to do something you may not want to do. Just keep this in mind if you decide to get involved."

I appreciated Albert telling me about his relationship with Joe, but I couldn't imagine what Joe would want from me. After all, I was just an eighteen-year-old kid. Besides, I didn't know why Albert was concerned. It appeared to me he made out well doing business with Joe. He owned half the gasoline filling station and it was busy every day. I finally knew why Albert stayed up all night to finish the repairs on the beautiful black Packard; it belonged to Joe, his silent partner.

Several days had passed from the time we had our conversation about Joe. I didn't hear back from Joe, but my curiosity grew about what he wanted from me. I couldn't wait to hear back from him; it would give me an opportunity to hopefully see Shannon again.

A few weeks later, Albert and I were driving into town one night to pick up supplies and parts when he told me Joe called and wanted to speak to me. He hadn't said anything earlier because he had hoped I would have forgotten about Joe. He said he was going to drop me off at the restaurant after we picked up the supplies for the gasoline filling station. He told me not to forget about our conversation if I were made an offer. I still didn't know what Joe wanted from me. As we pulled up in front of the restaurant, I told Albert not to worry. I would be fine.

When I stepped inside the restaurant, my heart began to race. I had already forgotten everything Albert had told me. There she was, standing down at the cash register counting the day's receipts. She didn't notice me when I walked in because she had her back to me. She shouted out, "Take a seat anywhere, I'll be with you in a moment." Her voice made me excited; I couldn't control myself. I wanted an opportunity to see Shannon again and now I had it. There was no one else in the restaurant besides us.

I sat at the counter right behind her and just waited for her to turn around. I wanted to act as if I wasn't excited to see her so she wouldn't know I had thought of her every day and night from the first day we met. I asked for a coffee, and she must have recognized my voice because she said, without turning around, "Where have you been? It's been awhile since you were here for breakfast. I thought you were from another town, someone just passing through."

I sat for a moment, then told her it was nice to see her again, too. "I'm not from Boston originally but moved here a few months ago from Canada with my brother. My brother is studying at Harvard, and I work for Albert at the gasoline filling station."

She poured me the coffee and looked over at the door. Shannon had beautiful blue eyes that glistened in the light from the lamp above us. I couldn't help but stare at her soft skin and long flowing hair. She asked me to wait a moment while she closed the curtains in the front windows and locked the door. The restaurant was closed now, and someone would be coming soon to meet with me.

While I waited, Shannon and I talked for what seemed to be hours. She told me she moved to Boston three years earlier from Ireland with her family. Her parents, a younger sister, and older brother continued on to New York to live with relatives while she stayed in Boston. She found work at the restaurant and moved into an apartment upstairs with another waitress. There were two apartments upstairs, but the other was always vacant.

While listening to Shannon, I started to wonder if Albert had arranged the meeting so I could be with her. After all, he did know her before. I also wondered if Albert really did have a meeting with Joe or one of his men.

Our conversation was interrupted by a knock on the door. Shannon walked around the counter and over to the door. She peered through the curtain and saw familiar faces. She unlocked the door and let the men in. Once they were in, she relocked it. She politely introduced me to the men and excused herself. She was going up to the apartment and asked us to turn the lights out when we were done.

Before leaving the room, Shannon turned to me and asked if I planned to come back for a meal. She said she enjoyed our conversation and wanted to learn more about me. She even suggested we meet one evening after work so she could show me around Boston. Before I could answer, one of the men said, "Of course he'll be back, how could he pass up a lovely dame like you?" We smiled at each other as she faded into the shadow of the back hall.

It was time to find out what Joe wanted from me. After my conversation with Albert about his business deal with Joe, I presumed he wanted to offer me something similar. But what kind of business did he have in mind? I had not shown any particular skills to him other than working with Albert. Maybe he was planning to help me get admitted to MIT? We already discussed how he knew everyone in Boston and how he had connections at MIT. I couldn't stop guessing. The men didn't come to the restaurant to have dinner.

There were two men, one of whom was Kieran, the driver from our first meeting, and the other introduced himself as Mr. Shamus O'Reilly. Shamus was wearing a finely tailored blue business suit and looked like a banker. As it turned out, he was. He worked for Joe at the bank across the street. Maybe Shamus was the same banker who met with Albert?

Shamus told me he knew of my parents' business and that Joe had met with them quite awhile ago. He said he knew of the very lucrative proposition offered my parents, but they turned him down. Shamus said he wanted to offer me the same deal but there would be specific rules that needed to be followed. Since Prohibition was still being enforced and organized crime groups controlled all transportation of liquor into the United States, I would be required to swear I wouldn't tell anyone who I worked for if I were ever stopped or questioned.

If I did say anything, all allegations would be denied and I would pay a costly price. If I followed orders, I would make a lot of money, more than I had ever imagined. Shamus said he would arrange for safe passage through customs at the Canadian border, but after that I was on my own. I would be told where and when to drop loads and how to make pickups for return trips to give the impression I was a legitimate businessman. More specific instructions would be provided if, and only if, I agreed to secrecy.

Since I couldn't get into MIT because of my lack of education and Max had to live off campus to help me, I realized I had nothing to lose. By now, I thought my parents' businesses may have been struggling to stay afloat, and the extra money could help tremendously. Besides, it was November of nineteen twenty-six and how much longer could Prohibition last?

Chapter Five

Six years had passed since Prohibition was enacted and by now many United States citizens were complaining about how the Government was spending a lot of money to enforce it. Yet, organized crime groups were still getting away with importing liquor and making tens of millions of dollars. Crime in the United States, especially homicides, had increased tenfold just because liquor was illegal.

I told Kieran and Shamus that I could be trusted with the secret no matter what happened and that I was interested in helping my parents. The only thing I asked for was a little time until Albert could find someone to replace me. Shamus said I would be paid twenty thousand dollars for each load I delivered. They'd give me one thousand dollars now and the rest would be paid when the first load of "hooch" arrived.

The twenty thousand dollars would cover the cost to purchase a truck, fuel, and liquor from my parents' distillery. After expenses to get started, the first load would make me a profit around fifteen thousand dollars. Now I understood why bootleggers were running liquor from Europe, Canada, and the Caribbean into the United States and why organized crime mobs defended the hold they had on transporting it. There was a lot of money to be made and the United States Government just didn't have the manpower to enforce Prohibition across the entire country.

Hearing the terms, I didn't hesitate to say yes. In nineteen twenty-six, the average worker made around fifteen hundred dollars a year. One load's profit would be enough for me. I wouldn't have to worry about my parents' businesses failing or having enough money to attend college to get a good job upon graduation.

After the meeting, Kieran unlocked the front door to let me out. Kieran said he would meet me outside to give me a ride home after he spoke to Shamus. As I waited on the curb out front, I wondered what I had agreed to. I knew what I was going to do was illegal; but for the amount of money I could earn, I didn't need to do it for very long. If I were careful, no one would know; and I would stop before there was a chance of getting caught.

Kieran pulled the automobile around front and Shamus turned out the lights in the restaurant. As Kieran drove me back to my apartment, he said that I had made the right decision and not to worry. He said he would always watch out for me and if I really needed help, I should contact him, and only him, for assistance. I felt relieved knowing Kieran could be counted on if I ever got into trouble.

When I returned to my apartment that evening, Max was busy studying. He had made dinner for us but had already eaten, not knowing when I would return home. I said I wasn't hungry but would clean up and put everything away so he could continue studying. He went back to his room, and I cleaned the kitchen before I went to bed.

The following morning, when I arrived at the gasoline filling station, Albert was standing in the office drinking coffee and waiting for me. He knew I met with someone from Joe's organization and was curious to find out what they wanted. Since I promised Kieran and Shamus I wouldn't tell anyone about the agreement, I told Albert everything was fine. I said I would be going back to Canada soon to help my parents with their business and that he needed to find someone to replace me. I also told Albert that I had a wonderful conversation with Shannon and that we had plans to see each other again.

With all the thoughts of working for Joe's men and going back to Canada, I had forgotten about Shannon. I needed to let her know I would be leaving soon but would be traveling between Canada and Boston on a regular basis. I was sure she would understand. It wasn't as though I was leaving and not coming back.

Albert said he didn't plan to replace me because he wasn't looking for anyone when he hired me. He told me if things didn't work out with the new arrangement I could always return if I needed work. He also said that he had grown fond of me and didn't just think of me as an employee. To him I was more like a family member since he had no family to speak of. I felt the same about Albert and assured him I would return from time to time to see him.

That evening I spoke to Max about returning to Canada. I explained that I was offered a delivery job driving goods back and forth between Canada and Boston. I said the money would be better than what I earned at Albert's gasoline filling station, and I would have the opportunity to travel. It would also give me an opportunity to see both him and our parents on a regular basis. Max agreed it would be good for me to go back home. He knew I was a little homesick, and he needed to live on campus to save money and to keep his grades up. I also assured him, any extra money I earned I would give to our parents to help with the businesses until he graduated.

Over the next few weeks Max and I spent as much time together as we could. I told him about Shannon, the waitress I met at the restaurant, so he knew for sure that I would be back in Boston on a regular basis.

During those few weeks, I had gone to the restaurant to see Shannon several times. As promised, she had met me after work to show me the city. We had such a great time. We really didn't do anything special or go any place in particular. We just walked around town and talked.

Shannon learned about my agreement with Joe from Kieran and said I could visit her whenever I was in town. It seemed as though she knew more about my arrangement than I did. She told me to call her to let her know where I was and what I was doing. She gave me the number to the pay phone in the restaurant and said she could hear it ring in her apartment if I called late. I could see in her eyes she really felt something for me, maybe the same feeling I had for her. She made me promise that whatever happened or wherever I traveled, I would call her to let her know I was all right. I promised I would.

It made me very happy knowing Shannon understood about the whole situation. As long as I knew she would be there for me when I returned from each trip, leaving was that much easier. During our last walk together, before I departed to Canada, we went back to her apartment. As we stood on the sidewalk I felt very awkward about saying good-bye but somehow managed to get up the courage to kiss her goodnight. As we drew closer together, I could tell she too felt awkward but the feelings we had towards each other helped us overcome our fears. We kissed passionately and held each other for several minutes as though we didn't want to let each other go. Just as we separated, it began to snow. We said our good-byes one more time and I turned to walk home.

That evening was magical, especially when it started to snow. I walked home thinking of her beauty and how I finally got to hold her in my arms. I had dreamt of that moment since the first time I met her and it had finally come true. As I walked home, I didn't feel the cold, the wind, or the snow on my face. Shannon had ignited a warm feeling inside me that never went away.

Since I would be going back home for a while, Max made arrangements with Harvard to move on campus. Harvard frowned upon first-year students living off campus, but because Max scored so well on his entrance exams and because of the situation with me at MIT, they reluctantly overlooked it.

The evening before I was to travel back to Blacks Harbour, Albert let me borrow the truck from the filling station. I needed the truck because I promised Max I would help him move into the dormitory on campus and since we rented the apartment furnished, we only needed to pack our personal belongings. We were able to move everything in one trip with the truck so we decided to go out for dinner that evening.

At the diner, Max told me he was proud of the fact that I had found work for myself at the filling station as quickly as I had and that I didn't get into trouble. He also said I was finally becoming responsible for myself and he had felt comfortable knowing I was thinking, not only of myself, but of our parents. He said my wanting to work as a delivery man to make more money to give to our parents was a good thing. He wondered why I had not thought more about getting into MIT but realized what I was doing was the best for everyone. It was comforting knowing Max didn't just think of me as a child anymore. After all, I was nineteen and I needed to take care of myself.

After dinner, we said our good-byes and Max gave me a few letters he had written to bring home. I dropped Max off at his new dormitory at school and returned to the gasoline filling station to return the truck.

We had a cot in the back of the filling station for nights when we worked late, so I just slept there that evening. It was so quiet at the station that I actually had a hard time getting to sleep. I kept thinking about helping my parents, making lots of money, and getting to see Shannon whenever I was in town. What more could I ask for?

The following morning Albert woke me up and gave me some coffee. We talked for a little while, but he knew I needed to get ready to leave. The train was departing from Boston to Bath, Maine, at ten o'clock that morning, and I didn't want to miss it.

Albert looked sad that morning. It seemed as though he wanted to tell me something but couldn't get the words out. He was acting the same way my mother did when I left Blacks Harbour. It was as though he wanted to come with me, to watch over me, but he and I both knew he had to stay to run the filling station. He knew I could take care of myself and that I would be back shortly.

51

Just before we left for the train station, Albert handed me a bag. He said he had made me something to eat for the journey so I wouldn't get hungry. He was acting exactly like my mother. I thanked him and shook his hand but he pulled me towards him and gave me a hug. He whispered into my ear to be careful and then let me go. Albert shocked me when he did that. For being such a stern man, Albert finally showed some emotion.

The train left Boston on time, as scheduled. My mind was racing with the thoughts of seeing my parents and friends again. I had lots of stories to tell about my adventures in Boston. I couldn't wait to tell Mother about Shannon and Father about the delivery job. They knew I was coming home, but I didn't give too many details about what I was going to do. I had to come up with a story to tell them. Selling the liquor for them was going to be the hardest part. They were already selling liquor to everyone they could, legally. I needed to come up with new customers to sell to and make them understand I wouldn't be breaking any laws.

While riding on the train, I began to notice the beautiful countryside. When Max and I traveled down to Boston, we were so excited about leaving Blacks Harbour and being on our own that I didn't really see what was around us during the journey. I was taking the train back to Bath and then would catch the ferry on to Blacks Harbour.

The train ride seemed a lot longer going home than when I first came down to Boston. I didn't remember stopping at all the local stations on the way to Boston. Since I didn't sleep well the night before the trip back home, I ended up sleeping most of the way to Bath. The train let out a loud whistle to announce our arrival as it pulled into the Bath station. The piercing sound startled me and woke me up. It was comforting to know I was almost home.

I walked from the train station to the boat dock. There I would board the ferry for the last leg of my journey. It was early December, the weather was bad, and the sea was rough. The ferry was late getting in, and it was posted that departure would be delayed. I waited across the street from the dock at a little eatery until the ferry arrived. It was already seven o'clock in the evening, and I dreaded the thought of a long trip in the rough waters, but it was the only way I knew to get home.

As I waited with no sign of the ferry's arrival, I decided to stay overnight and catch a ferry the following day. I asked around with the locals to find lodging and managed to get lucky. There was a room at an old house about six blocks away. The owner of the eatery said he didn't think the room was let for the evening. I left immediately before anyone else decided to stay. The moon was very bright that evening and its light reflected off the white snow. The streets were lit up from the white glow, which made it easy for me to find my way.

When I reached the house and knocked on the door, I met a tiny old lady. Her name was Mrs. Myers. She looked very frail but had a quick step when she walked up the stairs to the room. She said the room was vacant, and fifty cents for the night with breakfast in the morning was all she wanted.

As tired as I was, I handed her the money and undressed when she left the room. I fell into the bed and bundled myself under the sheets. It was chilly in the house and the wind whistled as it forced its way through cracks around the windows. In a few moments, my eyes closed and I fell into a deep sleep.

During the evening, while I slept, I had a strange dream. I could see fog floating above water as if I was standing on a boat dock and I could hear the sounds of the ocean breaking against a rocky shore. There were fog horns in the distance and the night was very dark. I couldn't figure out where I was but I did know I was near water. I could also see in the dream a light off in the distance rotating slowly.

The only thing I could imagine was that it must have been a lighthouse, but I still didn't know where I was. Suddenly, I began to move quickly as if the ground under my feet was racing forward, carrying me with it. As I rushed forward, I could see a light getting brighter and brighter as if it were moving toward me. After a few moments, I began to spin. I could hear shouts for help around me in the hazy night and then, all of a sudden, everything was dark and peaceful.

I woke up the next morning to a beautiful, sunny day. I still had the thoughts of the dream in my mind and wondered if it had a meaning. I didn't dwell on it too much longer because I could hear creaks coming from the stairs outside my room. It was Mrs. Myers; she was coming to wake me for breakfast. When she tapped on the bedroom door, I told her I was awake. She asked me to hurry so I wouldn't miss the ferry.

I washed up using an old ceramic bowl Mrs. Myers left outside my door. The water was hot and felt good on my face after the chilly night. I walked downstairs and met Mrs. Myers at the kitchen table. The house was furnished beautifully with decorative wood pieces. It looked so different during the day with the sun out. The evening before, when I arrived at the house, there was only oil lamps lit.

We talked for a bit while I ate the breakfast she had prepared. She was very inquisitive and wanted to know where I was going. I explained that I was on my way home to see my parents and had to leave soon so I wouldn't miss the ferry.

I stood up from the table and nodded farewell as I picked up my bag and walked to the front door. She told me that whenever I returned to Bath and needed a place to stay, I was always welcome. She said she looked forward to seeing me again. As I thanked her, I walked through the front door.

When I stepped outside, the sun was so bright I had to squint both of my eyes to see. It had snowed lightly the night before and the ground had a fresh coat of powdery white glitter on it. The snow crunched under my feet as I walked down the road to the docks.

The air was still and peaceful and the town was very quiet. When I arrived at the dock, I learned the ferry would be delayed longer so repairs could be made. Apparently, the rough seas the night before had caused some damage to the ferry. I hoped we wouldn't have trouble getting out, because I wanted to get home to see my parents.

I stood on the pier next to the ferry overlooking the ocean. There were many other boats around, mostly fishing boats and small cargo vessels. The water was unusually calm that morning, like the air. It was nice to feel the warm sun on my face as I watched men work to load and unload their boats. As I waited, enjoying the morning sunlight, I heard someone call out, "Hey, son! Aren't you Patrick's boy?" I looked down to see one of my father's old friends, Mr. O'Connor. He and his brother Robert had transported crops for my father many times. As I yelled, "Yes," he waved for me to come on board.

I walked down the ramp to the lower dock and up the plank to climb aboard. I threw my bag to one of his crew as he asked me where I was going. I told him I was on my way home and he offered to take me with him since the ferry was delayed.

Mr. O'Connor, or Captain John, as my father called him, said he was short a man and I could pay for the trip by helping his crew with loading cargo. He needed to make a few stops along the way to pick up more cargo before heading back to Blacks Harbour, but according to Mr. O'Connor, we would probably get to Blacks Harbour before the ferry. I agreed to help, so Mr. O'Connor told me to find a spot in the cargo hold for my bag and help the men finish loading so we could leave before the weather changed.

After finding a place for my bag, we loaded the last few items and left. The boat ran very rough but still had enough in her to get us back. As long as we stayed close to shore, someone could tow us in if we broke down. Captain John said he needed to make repairs to the boat's diesel engine but the repairs were expensive.

The cost of a new engine would be close to the cost of buying a new boat, he said. He had just made a final payment for a new vessel but needed to make this last run before the new boat could be picked up.

I asked him what he planned do with the boat when the new one was ready. He said he had already asked around and had no offers so he was going to scuttle it off the coast. The boat was sound and seaworthy, but it was old. I didn't think much of it when he said it but later thought I should ask if I could buy it. It would be perfect for what I needed to do, and no one would suspect Captain John's old boat of transporting anything illegal.

I told Captain John I was interested in buying his old boat. Since he and my father were good friends, he offered to sell it to me for ten dollars a foot. At just around fifty feet, it would cost only five hundred dollars. To save money I thought I could rebuild the engine with what I learned from Albert. I asked him not to say anything to my father before I had a chance to tell him first. Captain John laughed and agreed. I needed to find a way to get Father to let me keep the boat.

We made several stops along the way home, and the weather continued to cooperate. As we approached Blacks Harbour, the sun was just starting to rise. I could hear the men bustling on deck to get ready for our arrival. When I climbed up onto the deck I became very excited as I saw familiar surroundings. I could feel my life was about to make a major change but I couldn't understand how or why.

We docked the boat and unloaded Captain John's cargo for the last time. I paid him the five hundred dollars as he wished me luck with my father. The boat needed to be stored the rest of the winter, and I had to find a place to keep it. I grabbed my bag from the deck and made my way into town.

Gus had driven Mother to town in anticipation of the ferry's arrival. They learned the ferry would be late but hoped I would still make it to Blacks Harbour that day. While waiting for me, Mother decided to do some shopping at the general store. As I walked through town everyone was happy to see that I made it home safely. They had Captain John to thank. If it weren't for him offering me the ride I may have had to spend the rest of the winter with Mrs. Myers in Bath.

I found Gus sitting in the truck outside the general store waiting for Mother while she shopped. I walked up to him and placed my finger to my lips as I motioned him to stay quiet. I wanted to surprise Mother when she walked out of the store. I stood beside the front door of the general store and waited for her to exit. When she walked out, Gus just stared at her and didn't say anything. Mother thought this was odd because Gus was always talking. Mother turned back to look at the store and saw me standing there.

I quickly wrapped my arms around Mother and gave her a big hug. She was so happy to see me that a single tear rolled down her cheek.

She turned and wiped it from her face. She asked me to tell her all about my trip home, so I told her and Gus how I met up with Captain John in Bath and how he had offered to bring me back since the ferry was delayed because it needed repairs.

I asked how Father was and Mother told me he too was excited that I was coming home to help. I asked if there were any changes to the distillery and how the business was doing but she said she would rather wait for Father to tell me. I placed Mother's packages in the back of the truck and walked around to the driver's door. Mother slid into the middle and Gus walked around to the passenger side. Normally, one of us would ride in the back of the truck but because it was too cold, we all rode together in the front.

Chapter Six

The ride home with Mother and Gus was a lot of fun as I drove. The road was covered with ice and the sides of the road were piled high with snow. I hadn't driven in snow since I had left for Boston so I was a little out of practice. When the truck tires slid on the ice it made Mother very nervous. She wanted me to stop and let Gus drive but I told her not to worry. Although the road was slippery, the high piles of snow on each side prevented us from driving off into the brush or forest.

Gus and I laughed as Mother covered her eyes each time the truck swerved around a corner. The ride home from town would normally take about half an hour on a clear spring day but with the ice and snow we didn't expect to arrive at the farm for at least an hour. Mother had anticipated the long drive and purchased some food to snack on if we became hungry.

I hadn't eaten a good meal since I left Boston. I craved one of Mother's home-cooked dinners. She prepared a turkey for my arrival and kept it a secret to surprise me. Gus knew we would have a feast waiting for us at home and didn't say anything about it during the drive. We finally reached the house, and it looked exactly the way it did when I left for Boston. Since Father had the businesses there were plenty of men around to make sure maintenance on the house was kept up. Father was always making plans for some type of project, either around the house, at the shop, or at the farms. Since he worked so hard to build the businesses he always kept everything maintained in good order.

I pulled up to the front of the house and got out of the truck with Mother. I asked Gus if he would drive the truck around to the rear of the house. I grabbed the packages from the back of the truck and helped Mother up the front porch stairs. I could smell Mother's cooking as soon as I reached the top step. It was so nice to be home. As I entered through the front door, warmth ran through my body, that special type of thrill you get only when you know you're in a favorite place and everything is just right and peaceful.

Father was asleep in the front parlor with the radio still on. Sunday was his only day off, and he loved to listen to the big bands. He didn't hear us come in, so I walked quietly past him. Mother told me to wake him because she wanted Father to see me. It was early afternoon, and it had just started to rain.

It was a good time to get some rest, so I told Mother I was going to my room upstairs for a nap while she finished preparing dinner. Gus helped Mother unpack the bags and since I was going to nap for a little while, he decided to go home. Mother asked him to return around five to have dinner with us. After dinner would be a good time for us to catch up on what was going on in Blacks Harbour and what I did while in Boston.

I was so tired from the journey home that I fell asleep as soon as I lay down. Being in my own bed was so comforting. As I slept, I could hear familiar sounds like the music coming from the parlor and the rain dancing on the roof above my room. While I slept deeply, I had the same dream as I did when I slept at Mrs. Meyer's house. There was the fog, the water, and the darkness and the feeling of not knowing where I was. I woke up abruptly as if someone had shaken me. I looked around the room still dazed and thought I was dreaming of sleeping in my room. As my eyes focused and my mind cleared, I realized I was at home.

I could hear Mother talking to Father downstairs. Father must have awakened while I was asleep, and I couldn't wait to see him. I ran down the stairs and almost slipped on the rug at the bottom. Gus was back and Mother had already set the table for dinner. The music was still playing in the background and the rain continued to fall outside. I shook Father's hand but I really wanted to hug him. I couldn't remember ever hugging Father; even on the day I left for Boston, we shook hands. I was hoping someday we could break that cycle.

Father was really happy to have me home. While we sat at the dinner table waiting for Mother to serve us, he couldn't stop talking about all the plans he had for me at the distillery. He really didn't need any more help, and I knew he could barely afford to pay the staff he had. Gus's dad, Byron, had worked for Father for over fifty years and was now too old to be productive, but Father never thought of letting him go. Byron helped my grandfather run the farms before the distillery was started. Father owed a lot to Gus's dad, and I was happy he kept him on. If not, Gus and his family would have moved back to South Carolina, where they had relatives.

Mother finally finished serving dinner while Father, Gus and I continued to talk. She made my favorites—stuffed, basted turkey with potatoes, corn, carrots, and beans. Mother also made fresh biscuits with gravy and all the side dishes you could imagine. It was nice living on a farm. No matter how bad the economy, there was always good food to eat.

After dinner, I offered to help Mother clean up but she insisted I spend time with Father, telling him about my adventures in Boston. Father, Gus, and I walked to the parlor and found comfortable spots to relax. It would have been nice if Max was home. As strict and dominating as Max was, I wanted all of us to be together.

After being away for a while, I noticed how Father had aged.

When you're around people all the time you don't notice the gradual changes. But as soon as you leave for a while and come back, you can clearly see the changes. He was becoming old and moved much slower. His mind wasn't as keen and he kept calling me Max. I knew years of hard work and age were starting to take their toll on him. I dismissed all thoughts of what seemed to be a handicap with his aging mind. After all, he was a smart man and built great businesses in a place where there was hardly any work.

I told Father and Gus all about my experiences in Boston, starting from the day I arrived to the day I left on the train, a few days earlier. Father would fade in and out of sleep as though he couldn't keep himself focused. Gus, on the other hand, was as wide-eyed as a playful pup.

Gus had never left Blacks Harbour and listened with such intent as though he were reading a book. Unfortunately, Gus couldn't read. He had never gone to school because his parents needed him to work.

The day had grown dark and the rain continued to fall. Mother joined us in the parlor and Father had drifted back to sleep. I asked Mother how long Father had been like this, and she told me not to worry. She said he was just getting old and with Max and me away in Boston he had no one at home to keep his interest. I knew it was much more serious than that. I was glad I was home and that the events in my life had brought me back.

Seeing Father the way he was made me realize there was no sense in telling him about the boat I bought from Captain John. Even if I did tell him, I didn't think he would understand. It was obvious Mother was keeping everything together, the house, the farms, and the distillery. Since Father was such a disciplined businessman, the businesses primarily ran themselves.

I understood that's the way all businesses should run, like a clock. All you need to do is wind it up and let it go. Other than developing new products and selling, there was really nothing for Father to do but visit the businesses and oversee the workers. Everyone knew he was becoming senile but hoped either Max or I would return to run things.

I went to visit the farms and distillery with Father and Gus the next day. After seeing Father the way he was, I knew I needed to assure his workers all would be fine now that I was home. Since it was winter, there was not much activity at the farms, just maintenance of the equipment, and preparations for the next growing season. The distillery, on the other hand, was more active because of the approaching holiday season. Although there were no sales in the States, Canadian sales kept the distillery running at just under half our capability.

I explained to father's workers that I had some ideas to increase sales, but I would not be around all the time to run the facility. The men would need to continue as they were and let Father think he was still useful and still running everything. I didn't need to explain what I had planned because at that moment I really didn't know what I was going to do.

Father's workers felt confident I could keep the businesses running and all of them employed until Max returned from Harvard. I didn't want to tell Max about Father's condition because it would be hard for Max to concentrate at school.

Later in the week, Gus and I drove into town. I told Gus how I had bought the boat and made him promise he wouldn't tell anyone until I told him it was all right. I told Gus I had an idea and needed his help, but he couldn't tell anyone or else we would get in trouble with the law.

Gus was deathly afraid of the law because of the stories his parents had told him about the living conditions in the States for blacks as slaves before and during the Civil War. Blacks were beaten and killed even if they didn't break the law.

When we arrived in town and I showed Gus Captain John's boat, he couldn't stop laughing. In his own way he made fun of me and told me I spent good money on junk. Gus said everyone knew Captain John's boat was all used up and couldn't be used for anything but pleasure fishing. Even then, you couldn't trust the engine to get you back to shore and the boat was too big to row. I told Gus to have faith in me and his skill as a mechanic. When I told Gus that, he pretended to be serious but understood I really needed his help.

We made arrangements to get the boat dry-docked so we could work on it. After spending the money to buy the boat and paying for my trip and meals home, I still had about four hundred and fifty dollars from the advance I was given by Kieran and Shamus back in Boston. There was still plenty of money to pay for materials and workers if we needed extra help. The boat needed some cosmetic work so it would look like a legitimate cargo vessel.

We also needed to either repair or replace the diesel engine since it had very little life left in it. I anticipated painting the boat gray to keep it inconspicuous, and I wanted to strengthen the framework to handle the heavy loads of glass bottles. The weight of the filled glass bottles was going to be a problem and a powerful engine was needed to handle the load, rough seas and the trips back and forth to Boston.

During the next few months, Gus and I spent nearly every day working on the boat. Since it was the dead of winter, everything was slow in Blacks Harbour. It really snowed hard that winter and it was bitterly cold. We built a tent over the boat so we could work without the wind blowing on us all the time. We set up an old potbellied stove on the deck so when we needed warmth we could huddle around it.

The excitement of finishing the repairs by spring and getting the boat in the water helped us get through the harshest days. I had some of the men from the farm come down to the docks to help with the structural repairs and modifications. The men who worked for Father were real craftsmen and there were many out of work, and many old boat builders around to give us advice when we needed it. Repairing the boat started to become a major project. People from town who didn't mind working in the cold pitched in whenever possible. Most just wanted to see if we could get Captain John's old boat running again.

No one really knew what the boat was actually going to be used for. Everyone just wanted to help because they knew Father was ill. If I didn't keep the businesses running, many of the locals would need to find other work. In nineteen hundred and twenty-seven there wasn't much work to be found in Canada.

By mid February, we completed all the structural work. Gus spent several days deciding if we should spend money to repair the diesel engine or find a new one. Gus suggested we try to install the Liberty engine, the one we pulled out of the crashed *Boston* airplane. Although we never did get it to run earlier, Gus was confident we had a better chance with the Liberty than with rebuilding the old diesel. We went back to the farm and uncovered the engine.

While working for Albert at the filling station during my stay in Boston, I learned what I needed to get the Liberty engine running right. I thought it was ironic how I had learned to repair engines in Boston and the airplane we pulled the Liberty engine from was called the *Boston*.

Gus and I spent a couple of days in the shed at the farm working on the Liberty engine to get it started. After checking the fuel pump and filter system, we discovered it was working correctly.

Albert taught me, in order to get the maximum horsepower out of an engine, the timing, fuel, and air mixture had to be correctly adjusted. Without a repair manual, this required experience and special talent.

Adjusting the fuel mixture wasn't going to be easy. I needed to run the engine for at least ten minutes, and we couldn't run it at all without a cooling system. If we didn't keep the engine cool while running, it would seize and be of no use to us. The Liberty was designed with a liquid-cooling system to keep it from overheating under heavy use. I put together a makeshift system made from hoses and drums I brought over from the distillery. Now, if I could start the Liberty and keep the engine running long enough to finalize the adjustments we would have the power we needed for the boat.

I removed the battery and electric starter from the old diesel engine and fitted it to the Liberty. After some changes, I was able to get the Liberty to turn over. Now it was a matter of getting gasoline to the carburetors. Depending on the type of fuel we would use, I would need to readjust the mixture occasionally. Since I could never depend on finding the same type of fuel, I designed a mechanism which could be used for easy adjustments while the engine was running. I never imagined how useful this adjusting mechanism would become in later years.

With the battery-powered starter, fuel, and liquid cooling systems set up, we were able to start the Liberty. Although it ran rough at first, the cooling system worked perfectly. Once I fine-tuned the timing, fuel and air mixture, the Liberty ran very smoothly, exactly how I wanted it to. Gus and I just stared in amazement at each other. We couldn't believe how well the Liberty ran. Earlier, when we first removed the Liberty engine from the crashed airplane and Mr. Holland couldn't help us anymore, we thought we would never get it to run.

The Liberty engine was a marvel for its time. A twelve-cylinder, liquid-cooled gasoline engine that was very light in weight for its efficiency and power output. American automobile and engine producers manufactured thousands of Liberty engines to help the allies during the First World War. The Liberty generated around four hundred and fifty horsepower when fitted with a turbo-supercharger. There was no other mass-produced engine that could come close in matching the Liberty's strength and capabilities back in the twenties. Mostly used for airplanes, it had to be reliable.

After Gus and I got the Liberty running well, the next job was to transport it to the docks and get it into the boat. We used one of the tractors from the farm to load the engine into our truck. Once we had it at the boatyard we built an A-frame over the boat to winch out the old diesel and lower in the Liberty.

We modified the mounting platform in the boat to accept the new Liberty. Everything fit well and the installation went as smoothly as expected. I planned to use the same drive shaft and propeller originally installed for the diesel engine for the Liberty engine. The modifications to the boat's structure allowed us to secure the Liberty in place and attach the drive unit. Once we repaired and modified the diesel's cooling system to fit the Liberty, we were almost ready to get the boat back in the water.

Gus drained and removed the original fuel tank from the boat because it had diesel fuel in it. I designed a larger stainless steel tank for gasoline so we wouldn't need to refuel as often. Since the boat would be used to carry liquor, I preferred having more fuel than space for cargo. The only cargo we would carry would be what we needed to disguise the liquor.

After the diesel fuel tank was removed, I came up with another idea. We would design the new stainless steel tank to include a secret storage compartment for liquor bottles. If we were inspected by the Canadian Government or the United States Coast Guard, the liquor would be concealed in the compartment and hopefully, be undetectable. I wasn't really worried about being caught by either government. I was more concerned with Al Capone's men or the Purple Gang finding out what we were doing.

We finished fabricating the new fuel tank and installed it into the boat. Everything looked like we were ready to test it in the water. A majority of the thick harbor ice had melted so now we only needed to arrange to get the boat out of dry-dock and into the water. If we could get the boat out into open water, we could see how it would perform.

Chapter Seven

It was now early March, nineteen hundred and twenty-seven. The boat was completed and ready for the sea. The weather was starting to get warm enough to make plans for our first run to Boston. I needed to get the first load to Shamus and Kieran before Joe became impatient. I had about one hundred fifty dollars left of the advance they had given me. That would be enough to pay the boatyard for the storage, fuel for the trip to Boston, and a little left over for supplies. Although I made my own calculations, Captain John confirmed it would be at least three hundred and fifty nautical miles to Boston.

Captain John showed me how to register the boat and keep a log in order to be a legal vessel. We did have one problem; we needed a name for the boat. I wanted it to be unique, but simple. I didn't want to draw any unwanted attention with a flamboyant name if I could help it. Gus said I should name it after a woman and my first thought was to call it *Shannon*. It seemed appropriate at first, but I thought since Gus put so much work into it I would let him help me come up with the name.

Once the boat was back in the water, we pushed off the dock and anchored it near the tall reeds. We used the harbor dinghy to get us back to the docks; and as Gus rowed towards the shore, I turned back to see how the boat looked in the water from a distance. The sun was shining down on it as if the heavens were christening it with sunlight. Just then, under my breath, I whispered, "The *Black Duck*."

Looking at it in the reeds, the way it sat low in the water, reminded me of a duck. The grey boat with the black pilothouse resembled the body of a duck with a black head. Once again, I said, "The *Black Duck*." Only this time Gus heard me say the words. He looked over my shoulder and said to me "Yes, the *Black Duck*, that's what we'll call her."

Gus finished rowing us to shore, where we tied up the dinghy. We stood for a few minutes on the dock and realized what we had accomplished and that I now owned a boat named the *Black Duck*.

The next morning I drove to the distillery and had the men prepare five hundred cases of Father's best Irish whiskey so I could transport them in the truck to the dock. I told the men I had a buyer and would return in a week or so. No one really questioned what I was doing; they all thought I had my Father's permission.

Gus helped me with transporting the whiskey from the distillery to the boat at the docks. I told Gus that from now on he would work for me. He never really did get paid while working at the farm; his dad, Byron, was always given his earnings. Since Gus had never been out of New Brunswick, or far from Blacks Harbour, it didn't take him long to accept. He didn't care where we were going as long as we were together.

When we arrived at the dock, I told Gus to park the truck and to make sure the tarp on the whiskey was tied down well. I wanted to take the *Black Duck* out on the water to test her out before we made the long journey to Boston.

We finally had our chance to play with the boat and to see what she could do with the Liberty engine. We stopped at the harbormaster's house to borrow the dinghy again. The harbormaster was happy to see Captain John's old boat back on the water. The harbormaster and Captain John were old friends, and we wanted to show them we could be boaters, also.

Gus and I rowed out to the *Black Duck* and started her up. The Liberty was temperamental at first, but once it started to warm up it ran much smoother.

We towed the dinghy back to the dock and headed out for open water. I couldn't believe how well the *Black Duck* maneuvered through the bay and out past the first buoy. The tide was high that morning, so we didn't have to worry about hitting obstacles along the rocky shore. Dark thunderclouds were over us, but strong winds were blowing them away quickly.

Running the Liberty engine in the boat for the first time would be crucial in determining how far we could go before refueling. I designed the tank to hold eight hundred gallons of fuel, but adding the hidden compartment cut us back to five hundred and fifty gallons. We weren't sure of the speed we could achieve, but we hoped for the best considering the age of the boat and amount of liquor we would carry.

Without the load of liquor, the *Black Duck* sat high in the front and cut through the oncoming waves like a sharp knife. Little by little I slowly increased the throttle. The more fuel I gave her the faster she moved. I couldn't believe, even for her size, how much power and speed she had at only half throttle. With only half throttle we were jumping the short waves with ease.

I asked Gus to go below deck and check the cooling system and to see if the Liberty was running hot. I also wanted him to check for leaks in the old boat. The last thing we wanted was to lose a load of Father's best whiskey, or worse, our transportation to get the liquor to Boston. Gus came topside and reported no leaks that the bilge pump couldn't handle and that the Liberty was running cool, just the way we had planned.

Now that we were sure the *Black Duck* was a sound, seafaring vessel, I gave it full throttle. I looked over at Gus as he held on to the rail just outside the pilothouse door. Water was splashing up onto him and he had a big smile from the thrill. I, too, couldn't contain myself from enjoying the fast ride. We passed several other boats as if they were standing still. It felt as if we were on blades, skating over smooth ice.

I didn't want to stop the excitement, but we needed to return to the harbor and load the whiskey so we could leave for Boston the next morning. I motioned for Gus to come into the pilothouse so he could steer us back in. I reduced the throttle to slow speed and walked around the deck to see if there were any noticeable problems. Everything was fine and the bilge was working well enough to pump out the water faster than it was coming in.

We were all ready for our maiden voyage and only needed to load the whiskey and pack clothes and food for the trip. I stood on the bow as Gus steered us back to shore. I barked out directions, as a captain should, to keep us at a safe distance from other boats and protruding rocks. Gus handled the fifty-foot boat well. I was very surprised; he seemed so natural behind the wheel. It appeared as though he had done this in another life.

As we pulled up to the dock, Captain John and the harbormaster approached us. The harbormaster said he had timed us between the outer break wall and the first buoy. As experienced as they were in these waters and knowing the distance between the two points, they said we were moving at about twenty-nine knots. They watched us through the telescope and couldn't believe how fast we were moving for a fifty-foot boat.

Captain John, now knowing the speed of the *Black Duck*, made me promise I wouldn't become reckless on the water. He said the water can be your best friend one day and your worst enemy the next. To captain a boat as big as the *Black Duck* required clear focus of what you were doing, patience, a watchful eye, and a keen sense of direction. He also said he had known many experienced boaters who, for no reason, never returned to shore. Gus and I both promised we would be safe and always watch out for others.

Both Captain John and the harbormaster thought I bought the boat for pleasure and fishing but when they watched Gus and I load the whiskey from Father's distillery, they knew exactly what we were up to. No one said a word to us. No one really cared. It was illegal to buy liquor in the States but in Canada there were no laws being broken. As long as we paid our taxes for the exported liquor, the Canadian Government didn't want to know who we sold it to.

Once the whiskey was loaded, the *Black Duck* sat much lower in the water. Between the six thousand filled bottles and five hundred and fifty gallons of fuel, we added about four tons of weight to the boat. All that extra weight limited our speed tremendously. We would be lucky if we could do eighteen knots.

With our bags packed, whiskey loaded, and the *Black Duck* fully fueled, we were now ready to leave for Boston. I plotted our course, making sure we would stay at least twelve miles offshore until we were closer to Boston. Prior to the mid nineteen twenties, the international contiguous zone was only three miles.

Any vessel carrying and transporting illegal substances would sit just over the three-mile limit from shore to evade arrest and seizure by the United States Coast Guard. US citizens would easily take their own pleasure crafts, yachts, sailboats, or even rowboats out to the rum runners and try to return undetected or just drink at sea. Because it was so easy to get out to the runners at the three-mile limit and the Coast Guard could only watch helplessly, the laws were changed to extend to the twelve-mile limit.

If we traveled at a speed of around fifteen knots it would take the *Black Duck* at least twenty hours to get to Boston, if the weather and seas cooperated. We knew of the drastic changes in tide within the Bay of Fundy. With good weather, our only obstacle would be overcoming the inward current. Captain John said we were better off staying in the center of the Bay because there would be greater turbulence along shore. Our other option would be to depart when the tide receded and let it carry us along with it.

I only needed to do one more thing before we left; I wanted to call Shannon to let her know I was on my way back to Boston. Anticipating making the call gave me a strange feeling inside. I wasn't sure what the feeling was at the time, nerves, happiness, or fright.

Once I heard Shannon's voice on the telephone, I felt comfortable speaking to her. I told her of the purchase and repair of Captain John's old boat and how I was ready to depart for Boston with the cargo for Kieran and Shamus. Shannon asked me to stop in Rockport, Massachusetts, and to call her again before arriving in Boston. She said she would let Kieran know I was coming and that I would be traveling by boat to get there.

I knew I could trust Shannon to help, and I would need all the help I could get to keep from getting caught. I only wanted to make a few runs and then get out with the money before word spread of what I was doing. All I really wanted to do was help my parents not lose their business and get back to school.

Gus and I set out for Rockport with our new boat and cargo. It was much different, moving slower with a heavy load. The thrill we experienced when we tested the *Black Duck* was gone. Now we could only settle in for the long trip and any adventure that might come our way.

The seas were calm and based on the weather reports it looked as if we wouldn't encounter any changes. We navigated our way through the Bay of Fundy around the Grand Manan Island, making sure we kept the New Brunswick peninsula in our sights. In the calm waters we could see Yarmouth off in the far distance near the peninsula tip. We estimated we were approximately twenty-five miles northwest of Yarmouth and would soon be entering the Gulf of Maine.

The *Black Duck*'s Liberty engine had a powerful, smooth, muffled sound. The engine was running better than we had hoped, and we were hardly taking on any water. The constant purr of the engine was a soothing sound that slowly lulled us into a state of sleepiness. I needed something to keep me awake and focused. I didn't want to wander off course, and I promised Captain John I would stay alert and safe.

I brought fishing gear so we could appear as though we were out for a pleasure ride. When we reached the Gulf of Maine, we had been at sea for over six hours and still had quite a distance to go. I decided to cast a few lines overboard while Gus sat back in the pilothouse to steer our course. Based on our charts, we calculated we were about thirty-five miles southeast of Bar Harbor, Maine, well outside the twelve-mile continental waters of the US contiguous zone. We could barely make out the coast from that distance, because patches of light fog separated us from the shore.

I had quite a bit of luck fishing that afternoon. The time passed quickly as I reeled in lots of cod. I found it exciting because I had never fished in the open sea before. As children, Father would bring Max, Gus, and me into town with him so we could fish while he tended to business. Since he used Captain John to ship his products, we were always at the docks. The biggest thing we would pull in was flounder, and when you're seven or eight years old, even they seem to weigh twenty-five pounds.

The *Black Duck*'s deck was starting to fill with fish. I never thought to bring storage for our catch. I let Gus have his hand at fishing so I could steer the boat for a while. When I took over, I thought I saw something about two hundred yards off our bow but I couldn't make out what it was. Suddenly, Gus started to yell for me to look over the rear of the boat. We had come across a large group of whales with their cubs.

I reduced the engine to an idle and watched in amazement as one of the larger mother whales moved up alongside us. With her eyes wide open it seemed as if she were trying to communicate with us. Gus had thrown some of the cod into the water around the cub thinking it wanted to eat but they just passed it by. She was the biggest animal I had ever seen and almost as long as the *Black Duck*. She had to be at least forty five or fifty feet long but moved very slowly.

We couldn't waste time playing with the whales so I gave the engine a bit more gas and slowly pulled away. Later, Gus and I learned from Captain John that the whales we had seen were called "Right" whales. It was rare to see them in early spring and they usually migrated north to the Bay of Fundy after giving birth off the coast of Georgia and Florida. We also learned they were called "Right" whales by the old fishermen because they were slow moving, easy to catch, and floated when dead, making them the "right" whale to hunt.

With all the excitement from seeing the whales and the time spent fishing, I started to get tired. I needed to get some sleep if I wanted to stay alert and keep us on track. I asked Gus to take over for a few hours while I went below to rest. It was just after four o'clock in the afternoon so I asked Gus to wake me at six. We were just over halfway to Rockport and once I was rested I would take over for the rest of the trip. Just as it had earlier, the low rumble of the Liberty engine relaxed me to the point where falling asleep was easy.

When I awakened, it felt like I had slept for eight hours. I went topside to see where we were and found it was dark outside. Gus had also fallen asleep and didn't wake me like I had asked. I stopped the boat and woke Gus. I quickly looked around for landmarks but was still disoriented from the situation and needed to calm down. It was now midnight and if we had stayed on course, I estimated we should have been somewhere between Portland, Maine and Portsmouth, New Hampshire.

With a clearer head, I reviewed the charts. The situation wasn't as bad as I envisioned. There was no harm to the boat, and I spotted to our west what I thought was the Nubble Lighthouse. If it was Nubble, and I calculated correctly, we were within fifty miles of Rockport. I decided to anchor the *Black Duck* there 'til morning and wait for sunup to enter the harbor.

Gus said he wanted to let me sleep longer and was very apologetic for what he had done. I couldn't be angry with him. As captain of the *Black Duck* I should have let him rest first. I took responsibility for what had happened and told him it wasn't his fault. To make him feel better I said, "If I had steered our course as long as you did and had no one to keep me awake, I would have fallen asleep also." After some convincing, he agreed and decided to go below deck to prepare us some food.

While Gus was below, I sat on deck and enjoyed the beautiful, calm weather. There was a still, patchy fog around us and the air was cool. The sky was so clear above that the stars seemed as though you could almost reach up and touch them. Now I realized what Captain John meant when he said the sea can be your friend and enemy. We were fortunate that we hadn't run ashore, or even worse, hit another boat. Since the time we had left Blacks Harbour, we hadn't encountered any other vessels. I thought this was strange because we were never more than thirty miles from the shore. Maybe it had been because the larger fishing boats traveled much further out than our course had taken us.

Gus returned to the deck with supper for the two of us. We ate our food without saying a word to each other. Gus was still feeling uneasy because of what happened so I decided to break the silence. I asked Gus what he knew of his ancestors in the Carolinas and if he ever thought of traveling to see relatives there. He didn't know much of his past but did remember his grandmother telling stories of how her ancestors were brought over from Africa as slaves. There were no written documents of his past, and the only way most Negroes learned of their past was from stories told and passed down from generation to generation.

We both said at the same time, "I wonder what it's like in Africa?" We both laughed because we were thinking the exact same thing. Our laughter was broken by a scared look on Gus's face. I turned to look at what had silenced him and could see a large sailing ship coming straight towards us. It probably couldn't see us in the night fog so we began to scream and shout while waving our hands.

We couldn't see anyone on its deck and there was only one twinkling light on its center mast. We expected to be hit broadside; Gus continued to shout as I ran to the pilothouse. I knew we couldn't pull up the anchor fast enough, so I started the engine and swung the *Black Duck* to get out of the way. Just when I thought it was too late and there was no way the collision would be avoided, the big ship turned slightly north and narrowly missed us. As I peered through the fog, I could see the name of the vessel on its starboard side. The old sailing ship was called the *Isidore*.

As tattered as her sails were and the upper rail boards rotted, she looked to be over a hundred years old. Why was it at sea in the condition it was in, and why did it travel in the night fog with no lights? Even as close as it came to hitting us, we never heard or saw anyone on deck.

After all that happened to us in the last twelve hours, I started to think we would have been better off taking our chances transporting the liquor by land. There were more dangers at sea than I thought. If you were in trouble out here, there was no one to call for help. Only God could save you out here and from that point on I knew these trips weren't going to be any pleasure cruises.

That night, as Gus and I waited for our first sunrise on the *Black Duck*, we sat on deck and gazed up at the stars. We hoped the remainder of the day would be uneventful. We had enough excitement for one night. When morning did arrive, the sunrise was spectacular. As the sun peered over the horizon from the east, its rays reflected off the shallow waves and made a sparkle effect. I had never seen anything like it before. It looked like the million stars we had seen that night but only on the water.

With the sunrise came all the sea animals. The seagulls were flying overhead as if to welcome us that morning. They could see the cod on deck and were looking for a free morning meal. Gus and I threw a few smaller fish we had saved for bait up to the gulls. That was actually a mistake, because it only drew more seagulls to us. There were also fish flying just above the water all around us. You would think the gulls would leave us alone and go after them, but they just didn't.

Gus pulled up the anchor, and I started the engine. The Liberty was so reliable. Even during the encounter with the *Isidore*, the Liberty started on the first try. We checked for water down below as we waited for the Liberty to warm up and found everything was fine with the *Black Duck*. As the morning fog began to burn off, we started seeing larger fishing boats heading out towards deeper water.

We were only three hours from Rockport, and it was time to get to shore and make the call to Shannon. We headed south past Cape Ann and made our way into Rockport's harbor. I anchored the *Black Duck* offshore and the harbormaster sent a dinghy out to pick us up.

I asked Gus to stay with the boat and left in the dinghy. When I reached the docks, I walked into town to find a telephone. There wasn't much activity in town since all the fishing vessels left early that morning. I found the local general store and bought some food and a few supplies to take back to the *Black Duck*. The shop owner let me use his telephone to call Shannon. It was around ten o'clock, and I knew the restaurant in Boston would be busy. I let the telephone ring for a while, but I wasn't sure if Shannon would answer or not.

Finally someone picked up, and to my surprise, it was Kieran. He told me Shannon told him I was on my way and would contact her when I arrived. He wanted to know why I changed our original plan to come by truck and didn't let him know what I was doing until I left Blacks Harbour. I wasn't sure why he was upset with me since I didn't think he cared how the cargo arrived into Boston as long as I got it there.

He asked me where I was in an angry voice. I confirmed I was in Rockport at the general store. I explained the owner let me make the call, and I had what he was waiting for. He told me he knew the owner and to let him know he would be on his way up from Boston shortly. He told me to go back to the boat and wait outside the twelve mile limit. He would have someone come out to get me when he arrived.

As Kieran requested, I let the owner of the store know what he said. The storeowner said it was not a good time to be there and that the Coast Guard would be arriving soon to check the harbor. I walked back to the dock and had the harbormaster return me to the *Black Duck*. Gus was sitting in the pilothouse waiting patiently while I was away. He wanted to know when he could go ashore, and I told him not now and that we needed to get back out to sea. He had a puzzled look on his face so I said not to worry. We needed to wait for a friend and that they would send for us when the time was right.

I would soon need to tell Gus about the Coast Guard and that what we were doing was illegal. Once we were past the twelve-mile limit, I sat with him and explained the situation while we ate the food I picked up at the general store. I told Gus what was going on and that, if he decided not to be involved, he didn't have to make the trip anymore. I said I didn't want anyone to get hurt or arrested and since he was my best friend, I couldn't bear to think I would be the one to put him in harm's way.

A few hours later a small cabin cruiser pulled up alongside us and said he was sent by Kieran. The captain wanted us to follow him to a private inlet, where we could offload our cargo. We pulled up anchor and followed the cabin cruiser in. At the inlet there were several men with shotguns waiting on the shore. There was a truck waiting by the road; Kieran jumped out. He looked over at me and walked down to the sand. He asked me who the Negro was. I told him it was Gus, an old friend who rode with me on the boat, and he could be trusted.

Kieran told Gus to help the other men put the whiskey in the truck and for me to follow him. I nodded to Gus as if to say it was all right and that we were safe with these men. Kieran pulled me by my shirt sleeve as we walked along the shore toward a house. I wasn't sure what was going on. I thought Kieran was going to pay me but wanted to do it away from the group. Kieran pointed toward the house and said it was one of Joe's summer homes and it was safe to come to this inlet.

Kieran and I sat on a big log that had floated onto the shore. He looked me straight in the eyes and said, "From now on, whatever you do, you need to let me know. When I promised I would help you if you were ever in trouble, I could only do it when I know where you are, who you're with, and what you're doing." He went on to say that the Coast Guard had stepped up their patrols in these waters, anticipating more and more illegal rum running since winter was now over and the weather would be calm enough for the smaller boats to shuttle back and forth between the larger boats and shore.

Kieran also said that if I went to any port without him knowing, while carrying liquor, he might not be able to help. The only time I should go in was if I were empty or carrying legal goods. Kieran paid me the rest of the money owed but held back three thousand dollars. He said, since my agreement was to bring the whiskey to Boston, I would have to pay for the truck and the men needed to get it the rest of the way there.

I asked if he wanted another load of whiskey and if so, he would have to give me another advance. Kieran shouted as he pushed me away and said, "Get back to your boat and get to Boston. I'll tell you what to do and when to do it, not the other way around!"

Chapter Eight

After the *Black Duck* was unloaded, and all the cases were counted and tested, I went back to meet up with Gus. Sixteen thousand dollars was more than I had ever seen, or than most people at that time could earn in a lifetime. I placed fifteen thousand of it in a burlap bag before putting it in the hidden compartment of the fuel tank. With the lower deck of the *Black Duck* now empty, we headed over to Rockport to refuel. Along the way, with the boat much lighter, we enjoyed the speed and horsepower of the Liberty engine.

We planned to stay in Rockport long enough to refuel and pick up some supplies. Since Gus had never been away from Blacks Harbour, he wanted to walk around for a while. I think he just needed some time to get his land legs back. He and I walked for a few hours before we decided to go back to the dock. We stopped back at the general store along the way and I gave Gus twenty-five dollars to buy himself something. He picked out a few items but mostly purchased gifts for his parents.

When we returned to the dock, we found a few sailors standing around the *Black Duck*. At first I was worried that they had entered it to look for something to steal, but they were only looking for work. One of the older men asked if I were looking to hire, but I told him, "No." I said, "Maybe some other time, but not right now." He said he had lived in Rockport all his life and had never seen the *Black Duck* before. I told him I had just purchased the boat from a friend and we were testing its seaworthiness.

After learning the older sailor had lived in Rockport all of his life, I asked if he knew who owned or, had ever heard of the *Isidore* sailing ship. He looked at me with a peculiar grin and asked me where I had seen it. I told him about our mishap with Gus falling asleep and me waking about fifteen miles offshore near the Nubble Lighthouse. He said the last time the *Isidore* was seen was back in nineteen hundred and two, nearly twenty-five years ago.

He asked me how I knew it was the *Isidore*, so I described what Gus and I had seen. He acknowledged what I described was accurate, but it was impossible because the *Isidore* shipwrecked north of the lighthouse near Bald Head Cliff in eighteen forty-two. The Nubble Lighthouse wasn't built yet and if it had, maybe the *Isidore* would still be around.

The locals tell the story that, two nights before the *Isidore* set for sea, Thomas King, one of its crewmen, dreamt about a wreck and drowning sailors. King pleaded with the *Isidore's* captain not to go out in the stormy winter waters and hid when the ship sailed. Another story is told that one night before the *Isidore* set sail, another sailor had a premonition and saw seven coffins, himself being in one of them.

The morning after the ship set sail in a severe snowstorm, pieces of the *Isidore* were seen floating off Cape Neddick. Seven dead bodies were recovered and no survivors were ever found. The sailor who had the premonition of the coffins was one of the seven recovered. The remains of the sailing vessel and the captain were washed out to sea during that harsh winter storm.

The older sailor went on to tell me that some had claimed to have seen the *Isidore* with Captain Foss holding a torch near the main mast. He went on to say that there was no ghost ship and told me to stay off the juice while out at sea. I told him he was just as crazy as the story and that what we saw was real.

I knew what Gus and I saw was the *Isidore*, but why was there no crew on board? Maybe I just couldn't see anyone in the fog? I also wondered if the dreams I had at Mrs. Myers's house and my parents' home the day I returned from Boston were the same dreams the *Isidore's* sailors had. It just didn't make any sense to me.

I enjoyed talking to the older sailor and hearing his colorful tale, but Gus and I had to leave for Boston to meet with Kieran and Shamus. I also wanted to get there to see Shannon and take her out on the *Black Duck*.

We were able to power the *Black Duck* at full speed with no cargo. It only took us a little more than an hour to get to Boston from Rockport. We docked the boat in the old harbor and called Kieran to pick us up. Kieran wasn't at the restaurant and Shannon told us he would be in later. She said he told her to tell me that I was to go to Albert's filling station and wait for him there.

I wanted to see Albert anyway because he was the one who taught me what I needed to know to get the Liberty running. If it weren't for him, I would have never bought the boat; but he didn't know that. I knew he would be proud of the *Black Duck* and I couldn't wait to show him. I asked Gus to stay close to the docks so he could keep an eye on the boat. I told him not to worry and if anyone came around to cause him trouble, to just tell them he was a hired hand and the captain would be returning soon.

I walked over to the gasoline filling station to wait for Kieran. Albert was so happy to see me. He wanted to know why I was back, and I said Kieran instructed me to wait here. Albert said, "No, why are you back in Boston?" I told him it was part of the work I agreed to do for Joe.

Albert said Kieran had just left with some men after dropping off a few crates in the rear of the garage. I walked around back to see what he had left and found it was the whiskey I had brought down from

Blacks Harbour. I finally figured out the reason Joe really went into business with Albert; it was to use the filling station as a warehouse for liquor.

Since trucks would fill up every morning for their deliveries, it wouldn't create any suspicion for so many to come and go all the time. Now I knew why the filling station was always busy. All the trucks were probably Joe's men picking up the liquor to deliver to the local speakeasies.

Albert and I talked for a little while but he had to take care of customers. I told him I could help, but he asked me to sit in the office and wait for Kieran to come back. It was starting to get late and there was no sign of anyone coming to pick me up. I didn't want to leave Gus alone too long, especially since he knew no one here and was by himself watching the *Black Duck*.

Just before Albert was getting ready to close up the filling station, Shamus and Kieran arrived. Albert knew all along what they hired me for and didn't say a word to me about it. He understood I couldn't tell him about the relationship I had with Joe and respected my privacy by not asking. Kieran motioned for me to come to the car, so I walked over. Albert turned out the lights in the shop and left by the rear exit. I wasn't sure if he didn't want to interrupt us, or he wanted to avoid Kieran and Shamus.

When I reached the car, Shamus told me I did well today. He said he wanted another load delivered to the same spot Kieran brought me to earlier, the beach near Rockport. This time they wanted one thousand cases and would pay me forty thousand dollars. The plan was that I had to be back in two weeks, no sooner and no later. They would arrange for trucks to meet us and I was told to call Shannon before I left Canada.

With the thought of all that money and how it could help my parents, I said I could do it without really thinking about what I was agreeing to. Could the *Black Duck* hold that much liquor? How long would it take to get back down to Rockport with the extra weight? Would the Liberty hold up, and would the weather continue to be calm?

There were too many questions running through my head to think straight, but once I gave my word, I had to do it. I asked Shamus if he would bring me back to the docks, and he agreed because he wanted to see the *Black Duck*. We drove away from the dark filling station and headed to the harbor. While on the way, I asked Kieran how Shannon was. He told me to forget about that dame because, with what I was doing, there would be no time to socialize. He knew I felt something for her so he told me, in a joking way, that he was only teasing me. He wanted me to keep in touch with Shannon because she would be my main contact between us from now on.

When we reached the dock, I found Gus sitting there waiting patiently. As we approached, he stood stiff as though I was with unfriendly people. I told him everything was all right and that I knew these men. They were my business associates and the men we were working for. Gus, recognizing Kieran from the liquor drop off earlier, relaxed a little but managed never to turn his back on them.

We boarded the *Black Duck* and I showed Shamus and Kieran around. There really wasn't much to see but an empty boat. They wanted to know what we powering it with, and Gus told them all about the Liberty. Kieran was impressed with what Gus knew about engines and asked if he could see the Liberty. As they went below, Shamus held me back to stay on deck. When Gus and Kieran were out of sight, Shamus asked me if Gus could be trusted no matter what situation would arise.

I told Shamus about how Gus and I grew up together and that his father worked for mine at the farm. Shamus wanted to make sure Gus wouldn't tell anyone what we were doing, especially strangers. I assured him there was nothing to worry about, and between Gus and me, we would get the next load down to Boston without any incidents.

Feeling comfortable, Shamus called for Kieran to return topside. Apparently, Kieran and Gus had hit it off and there were no issues between them. Actually, they had much in common. Kieran had served in the First World War and knew quite a bit about Liberty engines. When they returned to the deck, Kieran said he had been given several Liberty engines as collateral for a loan and if I were interested, he would sell us one as a backup.

I didn't think another Liberty would do us any good so I declined. Gus then pulled me aside and said I should take Kieran's offer because after the laboring the engine went through powering the airplane there was no guarantee how long it would last. We walked back over to Kieran and Shamus and told them that I would accept the offer for another Liberty, and how much would he want for a new engine?

Kieran said he stored the engines at Albert's shop and I could pick it up the next day. He also said he would call Albert in the morning and give him permission to release it to me. Kieran still didn't tell me how much he wanted for the Liberty but with the next load paying me forty thousand dollars, money wasn't going to be a problem.

After Kieran and Shamus left, Gus and I decided to go on shore to get something to eat. As we were walking through the streets of the harbor, I saw the homeless children again. They were scavenging through the rubbish looking for food or anything of value they could sell. I explained to Gus how I had seen them while living in Boston and how I couldn't believe they had no one. I made a promise to Gus that night that somehow I would find a way to help the homeless children.

Gus and I slept on the *Black Duck* that evening after getting something to eat. I stayed awake for a little while thinking about how I could help the children, but the rocking of the boat in the harbor lulled me to sleep. Gus stayed awake that first evening. I wasn't sure if he was excited from being in Boston or if he just didn't trust both of us sleeping at the same time with no one to watch over the boat.

I woke up early the next morning and told Gus to get some sleep. I wanted to go and see Albert to arrange for the Liberty to be picked up but I also wanted to go to the restaurant to see Shannon. I walked to the filling station to see Albert around nine that morning. Albert said he hadn't heard from Kieran yet but he had no reason to doubt me. He walked me to the rear of the garage and showed me several Liberty engines. They were all in marked crates from the factory and bolted down to pallets. Each was covered with a cloth sheet soaked in oil to prevent any moisture or dust from accumulating on the engines. I noticed only one was equipped with a turbo-supercharger and that crate had markings for shipment to the Douglas Aircraft company.

I asked Albert if I could use the station's truck to take the crate to the dock so Gus and I could load the new Liberty onto the *Black Duck*. I also said I wanted to go to the restaurant to see Shannon and to get some breakfast. I couldn't bring Gus because he wouldn't be allowed in the restaurant. Albert told me he didn't need the truck until the afternoon and if I waited for the evening, he would close an hour early and help me with the crate.

Albert really turned out to be a great friend. He didn't have to loan me the truck that morning, but he knew I couldn't wait to see Shannon again. He gave me some change, asked me to fill up the truck with gasoline before I left and bring him back some breakfast. I asked what he wanted and he said Shannon would know. I gave him his money back and an extra dollar for the gas. I said I had earned some money, and I would treat him this time.

As I drove to the restaurant, I could envision Shannon behind the counter serving meals to all the patrons. I thought how all the work I had done on the *Black Duck*, the arrangement with Joe, and the need to help my parents were only excuses to come to Boston so I could be back with Shannon. If I hadn't agreed to bring the whiskey down from Blacks Harbour, I would have ended up working at Albert's garage or taking on some other job just to make a living. I knew with every run of whiskey came a new and exciting adventure. That was really the way I wanted to live my life.

Saturday mornings were a quiet time at the restaurant. Most of the local businessmen were home with their families on the weekends doing chores or at the horse races. There were not many shops in that section of town, mostly financial businesses, so I knew Shannon would have some free time to talk with me. When I arrived, there were only a few customers, so I sat at the counter.

I was happy to find Shannon was just as excited to see me as I was to see her. She gave me a beautiful smile and with her soft Irish accent asked how I was doing. We talked for a little while about my family in

Blacks Harbour. I had described my parents' home to her and the surrounding landscape. She said it sounded like the area she grew up in, back in Ireland. She wanted to know if I would take her there to meet my parents someday. Since her family all moved to New York, she seemed to be lonely for them.

Now, with the *Black Duck* as transportation, I could not only bring Shannon to Canada to visit my father and mother, but I could just as easily take her to New York to see her parents and siblings. Breakfast with Shannon turned out better than I expected. I promised her I would bring her to Blacks Harbour the next time she could take a few days off and that I would surprise her with a special treat when more time was available to travel.

I was really falling in love with this beautiful Irish girl. I never thought I would want to be with someone as much as I wanted to be with Shannon. I could see us together for the rest of our lives, but I needed to tell her how I felt before someone came along and swept her off her feet before I could.

It started getting late so I asked Shannon to put in the order for Albert's breakfast and I also had her add something for Gus. When she gave me the food, I apologized for rushing out but asked her if she would meet me that evening at the docks so I could show her the *Black Duck*. She said she would come by around eight thirty because she had made plans to meet with a friend for dinner. I waved goodbye as I hurried out the door. I needed to get back because Albert needed the truck.

On the way back to the station, I dropped off Gus's food. I told him I would be returning later that evening with the new Liberty engine. When I returned to the filling station, Albert didn't say anything about me being gone so long. He asked me to watch the filling station while he ran some errands. Since he was going to help to deliver the Liberty, I couldn't say no.

Albert wasn't gone very long and only a few customers came by. One customer, who recognized me from working there before, asked if I was returning to stay. I told him I was only going to be in town for a couple of days and I was just doing Albert a favor. I explained how

I had found another job and he wished me luck. He also said that he missed my good service and handy repair work. In a way, I did miss all the familiar customers and working for Albert. Maybe after I ran the next couple of loads for Kieran I would return to Boston and go back to working for Albert.

Albert closed up shop early that Saturday as promised and helped me load the Liberty into the truck. Albert said he had seen Kieran and Shamus while running errands, and they confirmed it was okay to take one of the Liberty engines. We returned to the boat and found Gus standing there talking to some of the homeless children. They were begging him for some money but he didn't have any to give. I told the boys, if they helped us load the crate onto the boat, I would give them each something for their help.

They eagerly jumped onto the truck to move the crate. With the help from the five boys, Albert, Gus, and I loaded the Liberty in no time. At first, I just wanted the crate left on deck, but Albert said it would be better to secure it below. If we hit bad weather, the sea water splashing on deck wouldn't be good for the engine.

After moving the Liberty down into the cargo hold, I pulled five single dollar bills out of my pocket. The oldest boy asked me to give him the money because the younger ones would spend it on treats. He said he would make sure they all had a good meal that evening and if anything was left over, he would split it between them.

When the boys left, Albert said I had been too generous. He said one dollar would have been enough for all of them to eat a proper meal. I said I had wanted to do something for the children, and I felt as though I hadn't given them enough. Albert laughed and said I couldn't feed the world.

Albert was very pleased with the *Black Duck*. He told me I had done a good job repairing Captain John's old boat and that the Liberty was an excellent engine to power it. After checking the work Gus and I did setting up the mechanism to adjust the fuel and air mixture, he was very impressed. He explained that if I made a few minor adjustments, I could set the carburetors to expel a large plume of black smoke out the exhaust if I needed to create a cover to escape any trouble.

He showed us what to do, and together, Gus and I made the changes Albert instructed. I wanted to finish because I knew Shannon would arrive soon. I wanted to take her for a ride, and I asked Albert if he wanted to come along with us. Albert said he had had a long day and needed to leave. I thanked him for all his help and for letting me borrow the truck that morning. He wished us luck and asked me to stop back to see him if I returned to Boston again soon. He knew I would be returning because of the arrangement I had with Kieran.

Soon after Albert left, Shannon arrived. She brought her roommate along. Carol was the friend Shannon had dinner with that night. I was relieved to know she wasn't out with a guy. Shannon knew Gus would be with me, and she thought if Carol joined us we wouldn't put Gus in an awkward position or have him feel left out. I gave them permission to come aboard as if I were the captain of a luxury yacht. They both giggled and held each other as they stumbled up the plank to us. Shannon reached out her hand to me so I could help her aboard. I caught her just as she began to slip on the wet plank and pulled her up against me.

Shannon brought us some leftover food from the restaurant where they had eaten. I wasn't hungry, but Gus didn't hesitate. She handed over the bag to Gus, and he thanked her for being so considerate. I showed the girls around the boat while Gus ate the roast beef. When Gus finished eating, he untied the lines so we could shove off. Gus was proud of the *Black Duck*'s speed and wanted every opportunity to show it off.

We set off out of the harbor to show Shannon and Carol what the *Black Duck* could do. Even with the new Liberty stowed below, the *Black Duck* had enough power to impress the girls. Shannon commented that the *Black Duck* had a lot of speed and agility for an old wooden boat. The girls were very excited to be out on the water and asked if we would take them to Long Point, near Provincetown.

It had been dark for more than an hour and I didn't know the waters around Boston. It was Saturday night so Shannon and Carol didn't need to be at work 'til Monday morning. As for Gus and I, we did whatever we wanted to do, so I pulled out the charts and set our course. As long as we delivered the next load to Kieran and Shamus on time in two weeks, no one would be expecting us.

We made it over to Long Point in about two hours. In the dark, as we entered Cape Cod Bay, the lighthouse shone bright enough to guide us most of the way. The shoreline at Long Point was very accessible, with no obstructions to the white, sandy beach. The night was cool with just a few puffy clouds as small waves splashed up on the beach. It had shown all signs of being a romantic night.

There were a few other boaters but plenty of shoreline so we could all keep a good distance from each other. We rode the *Black Duck* right up onto the beach and anchored her. It was mid-tide with the ocean retreating. I didn't want to stay on shore too long or we would end up being stuck there until the tide returned the following morning.

We left the *Black Duck* unattended while we strolled along the beach to the lighthouse. I had such a great time being with Shannon, and Carol kept Gus occupied. Carol had grown up in Boston and never traveled too far away. She found Gus very interesting with his stories about Blacks Harbour and Canada. He told her all about Max and me helping the pilots of the crashed plane. I never told anyone about the crash because I promised Mr. Hoffman I wouldn't, and my father was required to sign documents swearing to secrecy for the Douglas Company.

When we reached the lighthouse, the keeper let us walk up the steep steps to get a good view of the ocean and beach. The keeper explained to us the thirty-eight-foot brick tower was fairly new and was built just fifty-two years earlier. In eighteen seventy-five, the older structure had been replaced because the pilings the old lighthouse stood upon were rotted. If a heavy storm hit the area, the older lighthouse was in danger of being wiped out. The keeper also told us that at the time of the rebuilding a twelve-hundred-pound fog bell had also been installed to assist the big ships navigating into Cape Cod Bay during heavy fog.

With only a few clouds that evening, the clear sky allowed us to see hundreds of thousands of stars above us. The beach was very pristine. Considering the Pilgrims had visited the Point nearly three hundred years earlier, and in spite of the many recent visitors from the New England area, the Point still retained its beauty and natural state.

I asked the girls if they wanted to go back to Boston before it got too late. I didn't want to get stranded on shore and risk damage to the *Black Duck*. Shannon asked if it would be all right to anchor the *Black Duck* offshore and spend the night on the boat. Shannon and Carol said they wouldn't mind sleeping in the bunks below if Gus and I didn't mind sleeping on deck. Not wanting to go back to Boston so soon, Gus and I agreed to sleep on deck.

As it was, I wanted as much time with Shannon as I could get, and I really needed to get a good night's sleep before returning to Boston. The last couple of days were very exhausting and the trip home to Blacks Harbour would require me to be alert. I didn't want to go through the same ordeal where Gus and I both fell asleep on the way down from Canada with no one manning the *Black Duck*.

Chapter Nine

It became evident Carol started taking a liking to Gus. As we all walked back to the boat, I could see she was teasing him like a little schoolgirl. She poked and tickled Gus as if she wanted him to do the same back to her. Gus and Carol ran ahead of Shannon and it appeared as though they wanted to be alone for a little while. I didn't mind at all because it would give me time with Shannon. We reached the *Black Duck* and I called up to Gus to throw us a blanket because the wind kicked up slightly and the night air started to get a little chilly.

I think the girls had somehow planned to get Gus and me alone with each of them for a little while. Shannon and I took the blanket from Gus and turned back towards the lighthouse. We told Gus and Carol we would be back in an hour because we needed to shove off before the tide went out. With Carol tugging at Gus's arm, he looked at us with a big smile. Gus winked as if to thank us for letting them have the boat to themselves for a little while. I saluted up to him and draped the blanket over Shannon's shoulder as we walked away.

I finally had the chance to get close to Shannon. We sat in the sand a few hundred yards from the boat with our silhouettes lying on the sand beside us from the light of the moon. I wished it was us lying together on the sand, and I wrapped the blanket around us as we cuddled closer together for warmth. I had envisioned this moment for a long time and didn't want to waste the time with small talk. I asked her what she thought of the *Black Duck*, and she immediately changed the subject to us. She said she had missed me while I was away in Canada during the winter. Shannon said she wanted me to come back so I could keep her warm on those cold, lonely nights. I told her I had felt the same way while I was away and couldn't wait to return to Boston so I could be with her.

I realized that the girls had set us up so Shannon could have the opportunity to talk to me. The restaurant wasn't a good place to talk about our feelings because there were always people there. Since Shannon shared the upstairs apartment with Carol, it made it difficult to invite me up for time together. Now that Gus was in the picture, and he would be making deliveries with me to Boston, I could always let Gus and Carol stay with the *Black Duck* so Shannon and I could be alone.

Shannon placed her hands behind my neck and slowly pulled me towards her. I could see in her eyes she wanted me to hold her close and kiss her, so I did. The feeling I had the first time we kissed at the restaurant returned. It reminded me why I had agreed to the arrangement with Joe. It wasn't for the money; it was because I wanted a reason to come back to Boston to be with Shannon.

We continued holding each other and immersed ourselves in the warmth from our bodies. I didn't want to let her go. I wanted her to be with me the rest of my life. I could feel the heat rush through my body as we continued to hold one another and gaze quietly out over the bay. Soon the sun would be coming up and we would need to get back to the boat. I didn't want that moment to end.

We slowly rose from the sand and made our way back to the *Black Duck*. There were no signs of Carol and Gus so I asked Shannon to go below to find them. When she came topside, she said they were both asleep and she didn't have the heart to wake them. Shannon said they looked so comfortable and peaceful together and she would sleep up on deck.

I pulled up the anchor and backed the *Black Duck* off the beach. I turned the boat around as I looked for a spot in the bay. Gus must have awakened when I started the engine because he came to the pilothouse to see if I needed help. I told him everything was all right and to go back to sleep. I positioned the boat and dropped the anchor so Shannon and I could watch the sunrise.

It was a beautiful morning for several reasons. We stared to the east as the sun emitted colorful rays up toward the heavens. It was a sight that's been etched in my mind from that moment on. I have never forgotten that beautiful view or, that day.

I had been up for twenty-four hours now and was straining to keep my eyes open. Although we wanted to stay awake, Shannon and I eventually dozed off. I had such a peaceful sleep holding Shannon in my arms. Just as we did on the beach the night before, we held each other tightly.

I was awakened by the rocking of the *Black Duck* and loud seagulls flying overhead. When I looked out, there were several other boats anchored around us. It was Sunday morning and the bay started to fill with weekend boaters. It started getting a little too crowded for me. I thought now would be a good time to head back to Boston.

Gus and Carol were still below deck when I woke up. I could hear them talking to each other. Shannon was asleep, and the sun was starting to beat down on her. With her milky-white skin she would get seriously burned if she stayed in the sun. I pulled the tarp open up above her, which made enough shade to protect her.

With Shannon covered, and Gus and Carol still below, I stripped down to my shorts and dove in the bay. I hadn't bathed since Gus and I left Canada, and the cold March water felt very refreshing. The water was so crystal clear that I could see the ripples in the sand thirty feet below the boat. Soon after I dove in, Gus and Carol came up to the deck and followed my lead. They soon jumped in to refresh themselves.

Swimming in the bay was very refreshing to all of us. I asked Carol if I should wake Shannon, and she told me to let her sleep. Carol said Shannon had not been sleeping well since I left and could use the rest. I stayed in the water for a little longer and decided I had had enough. Gus and Carol couldn't keep their hands off each other and watching them made me want to be back with Shannon.

Just as I climbed back on the *Black Duck*, we were approached by a US Coast Guard cutter. They said they were checking boat registrations, but I presumed they were looking for rum runners. Most of the boats around us were yachts, which made the *Black Duck* stand out. Since we were the only boat with Canadian registration, they asked if they could board our vessel and have a look around. I had nothing to hide so I gave them permission.

I woke Shannon to let her know what was going on and they proceeded to go below deck. All they found was the Liberty engine I purchased from Kieran. I was asked to show the receipt for the engine and since I couldn't, I was told to follow them back to Boston. I had a feeling, even though we weren't doing anything wrong, they would find something to harass us about.

When the Coast Guard captain was told we would be following them back to Boston, he came aboard the *Black Duck* to ask me additional questions. Once he was on deck he saw Shannon and approached her. They spoke for about fifteen minutes alone and the cutter's captain walked back over to me. Apparently, he and Shannon knew each other and she persuaded him to let us go about our business. The cutter's captain told me I was lucky that Shannon was with us or else, if I couldn't prove I purchased the Liberty legitimately, he would have confiscated the cargo.

The captain and his men returned to their boat and headed south. Once the Coast Guard was out of sight, I started up the *Black Duck* so we could go back to Boston. The mood on the boat had changed dramatically. One moment we were all having a wonderful time playing, laughing, and getting to know each other, and the next minute we were being questioned by the Coast Guard.

I wondered how Shannon knew the Coast Guard captain and

what it was she said to him to let us go. Whatever she said, I was thankful she intervened. I wasn't worried about having the Liberty engine confiscated because I could have purchased another from Kieran. I was more concerned about them finding the money I received from Kieran and Shamus for delivering the load of whiskey.

If they found the burlap bag with the fifteen thousand dollars in the fuel tank's hidden compartment, it would have certainly raised their suspicions about whether we were involved in anything illegal. I couldn't take any more chances like that and let my guard down. Now that the Coast Guard knew of me and that I was from Canada, you could bet they would be keeping an eye out for me.

Shannon finally approached me in the pilothouse and told me the captain, Peter Scully, was an old friend who she had met when she and her family first arrived in Boston. "Peter knew my parents had moved on to New York and told them, before they left, that he would watch after me. I think he feels obligated since he promised my parents to keep an eye on me." She said Peter had made many advances towards her, but she wasn't interested in him.

Peter had been in the Coast Guard for several years and planned to make a career of it. She went on to say she didn't think she could live as a captain's girlfriend or wife since he was required to be discreet about his activities in the Coast Guard. He would always be under the scrutiny of the public and Government as a captain. Any controversy could jeopardize his career and she didn't want that pressure.

I felt relieved when Shannon told me how she knew the captain and why he didn't make us follow him to Boston. I also felt better knowing she had no real feelings for him other than as a friend. It still left many unanswered questions about how Shannon felt about me. I now knew what she didn't want, but I didn't know what she did want. Somehow I needed to find a way to get Shannon to want me so we could always be together.

After our conversation, I thanked Shannon for being honest with me. The fact that she came to me to tell me how she felt, without me having to ask her, was a good sign. We put our arms around each other as we headed back to Boston and enjoyed the rest of the time we had with each other that day.

When we arrived back at Boston Harbor, Shannon told me she had had a wonderful time and that she wanted to get together again soon. I told her Gus and I would be back in two weeks with the next load for Kieran and that I was instructed to call her before we left Canada for the return trip. She told me she knew about the next load and would wait for my call. I asked her not to mention anything about the Coast Guard incident to Kieran or Shamus. If they were to find out, it would cause problems and may end the business partnership.

She promised she wouldn't say a word and said she would tell Carol to keep it to herself also. She said Carol could be trusted and that I shouldn't worry about it anymore. Shannon also told me she would have a surprise for me when I returned and then gave me a kiss for good luck. I watched as Carol and Shannon walked away and wondered what the surprise could be.

It was getting late and Gus and I hadn't eaten since the night before. We walked into town to buy some groceries to bring back to the *Black Duck*. We would need to leave for Blacks Harbour early the next morning and the supplies would allow us not to stop along the way. Once we fueled up in the morning there would be no reason to stop until we reached home.

The next morning the weather wasn't even fit for waterfowl. The winds had picked up and the rain was coming down hard. There were whitecaps in the harbor, which was unusual since it was protected by the outer break wall. We decided to take our chances and headed home to Canada anyway.

With the *Black Duck*'s length just around fifty feet and the Liberty engine seeming more and more reliable; the storm and waves didn't present any threat. I worried more about making sure we stayed on course. If the water continued to be rough we could always find a safe haven in a harbor along the way and drop anchor until the weather cleared. The extra weight of the crated Liberty, below deck, centered in the hull and acted as a ballast to keep us steady in the rough waters.

After a few hours of riding out the storm the weather finally subsided. The rest of the trip home was easier since our only cargo was the spare Liberty. As we neared Portsmouth, New Hampshire, I noticed a vessel resembling a Coast Guard cutter similar to the one that searched us at the Long Port lighthouse. It was gaining ground on us as if it wanted to follow where we were going. I had no liquor on board but still didn't want to let them get too close so I increased the throttle slowly up to full speed.

We began to pull away from the cutter, leaving it further and further behind. I knew that wouldn't be the last we would see of them, but I couldn't believe the Coast Guard vessel didn't have the ability to keep up with us, considering they were commissioned to hunt down and catch anyone suspected of being a rum runner. The way the Black Duck was set up with the Liberty, we realized we had a unique capability and didn't have to worry about the Coast Guard catching us as long as our cargo hold was empty. If we came across them with a full load of whiskey I don't think we would be able to shake them off as easily as we did this time. We needed to be very careful when traveling during daylight.

We continued for a while traveling up the New England Coast and decided to stop back in Bath, Maine. There was a men's clothing store in town near the docks and I needed some new clothes before going home. I hadn't changed in a while and I smelled like fish and oil. Gus needed a bath worse than I so we found our way to shore and docked at the pier where I had met Captain John during my last trip home.

After docking the Black Duck we walked to Morris Povich's Clothing and Shoe Store and purchased a few new shirts and pants. It was nice having money to do as I pleased and to take care of my best friend, Gus. I'm not sure if he ever had new clothes to wear. One thing I made sure of though; I made sure Gus had a good pair of shoes. I couldn't believe the look on his face when he tried them on. Every time I did something which seemed insignificant to me, I realized Gus was experiencing it for the first time.

Leaving Blacks Harbour for the first time in his life was having a profound effect on Gus. I guess when I left for Boston the first time others saw the same effects traveling away from home had on me. Not that I was a seasoned traveler or anything, I just looked at the world from a different perspective once I left Blacks Harbour.

I began to learn my way around Bath more easily and knew we would be spending more time there if the whiskey orders continued. After we made our clothing purchases I walked with Gus up to Mrs. Myers's house. I hoped she still rented rooms. I'm sure she would let us bathe and change for a dollar or two. I felt we could always count on her to give us a warm meal, bath and bed when we needed it.

When we arrived at the house, Mrs. Myers was in the yard planting some flowers. The last time I was here it was the beginning of winter. The house and yard looked so different in the spring. It was nice to see Mrs. Myers again. She asked how I was and asked if I needed a room. I nodded yes and introduced her to Gus. Afterwards she led us into the parlor and politely asked us for one dollar. She wasted no time in making sure she was paid first. We didn't care about the cost because her hospitality was so sincere. She really cared for us, like we were her own family.

Chapter Ten

Gus and I wasted no time in finding our rooms so we could relax for a while. Mrs. Myers went back outside to finish planting her flowers. I wasn't sure which was worse, being hungry, dirty or tired. Out of the three I would have preferred being hungry. Usually you can find a decent place to eat, but it wasn't always easy finding a quiet place to sleep or a clean place to wash up.

Traveling to Boston and back with little rest and no place to bathe was going to become common during the trips while running the whiskey. As long as we stayed alert we could avoid getting caught by the Coast Guard. After all, we had a fast boat so it was only a matter of keeping our eyes open for any trouble.

Gus washed up first and took a long time doing so. I don't know when the last time he had a hot bath. In my house, back in Blacks Harbour, and the apartment in Boston I had running hot water. Gus's house didn't even have indoor plumbing. I didn't think much of it growing up. I knew Gus and his family had to boil water to bathe but just assumed someday they would have plumbing installed. Now I know there wasn't enough money to do it. I made a promise to myself after that day that I would change that when we returned.

After cleaning up we put on our new clothes and went downstairs to find Mrs. Myers cooking dinner. It wasn't much but considering we paid just a dollar we were grateful for whatever she made us. After dinner we could hardly keep our eyes open. A warm bed and clean sheets was very comforting especially because since leaving Blacks Harbour we only slept on the boat.

As I lay down in bed I started to think about what I really wanted to do. I needed to put a plan together if I was going to continue bringing illegal liquor to Boston. If I wanted to help my family, the people who worked for us back in Blacks Harbour and the children I saw on the streets in Boston, I'd need to get myself in order. After the next load I'd have plenty of money to pay any outstanding debts my family had and use the rest for myself.

Now I wanted to get back to Blacks Harbour. I wanted to do lots of things with my life but I needed a plan. I slowly drifted off to sleep and continued to think about what I needed to do. It was as if my mind had taken over my thoughts and gave me direction as to what I had to do. As I slept I continued to see what I would be doing. It seemed as though I had been at a theater all evening and watched my life's story played out before me. It became crystal clear what I needed to do.

The next morning I was very rested and relaxed. Waking up to the soft sheets reminded me of being in my own bed at home. The comfort we feel when we return to our own bed is as individual as the people we are. There is no other feeling like it.

I could hear Gus and Mrs. Myers moving around in the house. It was time to get up and out and get back home. I thought a little about what I saw in my sleep. I didn't say anything to Gus or Mrs. Myers about the plan. I just kept it to myself and wondered if it would all come true. There was only one way to find out and that was to live it.

After breakfast we walked back to the *Black Duck*. It would take about ten hours before we would return home. With a good night's sleep the trip home would be easy. The seas were calm again and hopefully it would stay that way.

The *Black Duck* started right up as usual. We were very lucky we had no problems with the boat. Considering the age and condition of the boat when we bought it from Captain John and the fact we thought we would never get the Liberty running we could only thank God for our good fortune.

We topped off the fuel tank at the dock before heading out. I wanted to make the last leg of the trip without stopping. I let Gus take the helm to guide us due east. I preferred being out past the twelve-mile limit to get used to navigating from that distance. Captain John told me to remember landmarks from certain distances so I could estimate where we were at all times. Traveling by landmarks would only be useful during daylight hours and only if the weather was clear. From now on my plan would be to always travel at night.

Once we reached the outer edge of the twelve-mile limit we headed due north. From there on, our course would not change much. If I calculated correctly we would be home just before sundown. Gus and I took turns steering and looking out for any obstacles. About five hours into the trip I prepared lunch for the two of us and we sat quietly while we ate. The trip was almost half over and soon we would be home again.

We reached the Bay of Fundy and could see Nova Scotia over our bow. We were in familiar waters now and nothing could stop us. I increased the throttle to full and the bow of the *Black Duck* lifted slightly out of the water as we sped forward. The thrill was there again! We both had that excited look on our faces as we cut through the waves. We were now safely approaching home.

When we reached the docks the only person around was the harbormaster. All the other fishing vessels were still out at sea and would be returning soon. It was around five o'clock in the evening and if we hurried we could catch a late dinner at home before Mother put everything away.

We anchored the boat and locked her down. We didn't need to worry about anyone messing with it when we were home. Gus and I rode the dingy to the dock, loaded our gear in the truck and headed home for a much deserved home-cooked meal and some rest. We didn't have to be back in Boston for another two weeks so all I needed to do was make sure my family was fine and the businesses were in order.

I had wanted to meet with the local banker and find a lawyer to help straighten out all our legal affairs to show Max I could handle the work and help Mother while Max was away at school. I presumed once he returned he would take the businesses under his control and I would have little to say about it.

Driving the old road home seemed like it took forever. I guess when you long to be somewhere the trip always seems longer getting there. When we pulled into the yard Mother had just helped Father out onto the porch so he could sit for a while and enjoy the night's cool air.

Mother was always excited when we returned home but this time she showed little emotion. It appeared Father's health had taken a turn for the worse. He became less and less aware of his surroundings and who everyone was just in the short time Gus and I were away. Mother went back into the house to prepare leftovers for us while I sat out on the porch with Father.

At first Father didn't seem to recognize me because he called me Max. At least he knew I was one of his sons. When I didn't respond to being called Max Father looked up and realized who I was. Just then a tear rolled down his cheek. To this day I don't really know why he cried. Was it because he was happy to see me home? Was it because he didn't recognize me or was it because he realized that the smart, strong, caring man that he once was, was starting to fade away?

I'll never know what Father was thinking that day but I was happy I had the opportunity to see him as himself because shortly thereafter it became more and more difficult for him to remember anything, let alone us. Mother now needed help caring for Father because it was going to become a full-time job.

After we ate the leftovers Mother prepared, we sat and talked for a little while about what help she would need. I told her financially we were secure but I wouldn't be staying home for long. I discussed with her the opportunities I had in Boston and the plans I had made to speak with Father's banker to settle any debt.

Gus left immediately after dinner so he could go home to see his parents. I didn't know if he told anyone where he was going or that he would be traveling with me back to Boston. I'm sure Mother had an idea he was with me and told his parents so they wouldn't worry. They knew I would always watch over him and would never let anything happen to Gus. After all, we knew each other from childhood and he was my best friend.

That evening I was too excited to go to sleep after traveling for the entire day. I thought I would fall asleep easily but couldn't. I still had the thought of Father's condition in my head and couldn't get over how much his mental capacity had deteriorated. I also worried how Mother would take care of him while Max and I were away.

If I could take care of all the financial concerns Mother would be free of managing that part of the business. The way Father had set up and conducted the businesses we knew he didn't need to be leading them in order for them to succeed. I eventually did fall asleep with all these thoughts running through my head.

The following morning I woke up late. It was around ten o'clock and that was unusual for me because I always got up as the sun came up. The house was very quiet that morning. I presumed with Max and me away and Father as ill as he was there was no more activity around the house. When I went downstairs Mother had already left the house for the day. I believe she must have felt, with me home now, she could leave Father alone with me and get some chores and shopping done.

I too wanted to go into town to meet with Father's banker. I wanted to leave, but I knew Mother would be angry if I left Father home alone by himself. I took a walk around the house to check out the condition and everything was fine. The workers had made sure there was nothing Father had to do so he could rest. I was happy to see Mother did have help around the house, at least the outside and land didn't need to be tended to.

I encouraged Father to walk with me around the house. He did so but reluctantly. He was content sitting on the porch but I wanted his company and I wasn't one to just sit around. We enjoyed the rest of the morning and half the afternoon together. I could see in his eyes he was happy with me being home. Or it could have been just because he was with someone else other than Mother.

Mother arrived at home around two thirty that afternoon with groceries for the house. I asked Mother who had done the shopping for her while I was away and she replied Gus's mother had picked up items when she went shopping. I asked Mother if she told Gus's mother he was with me and she said yes. She also said Gus's mother wasn't sure if Gus had left with me but since he didn't show up at the farm for a couple of days and it had been around the time I left she had hoped he was with me. Not just because she was worried about Gus but because she had hoped I didn't make the trip to Boston alone.

I helped Mother bring the groceries into the house and told her I was going to take the truck into town. She didn't ask why, she just asked me to be home for dinner. I left shortly thereafter and drove down to the docks. I rowed out to the *Black Duck* and retrieved the money I had left in the boat. I wasn't sure how much Father owed the bank so I brought the entire fifteen thousand dollars. Whatever I didn't need for Father's debts I would deposit into an account for myself. It was more money than I had ever seen and I didn't want to carry it around.

When I arrived in town it was close to the bank's closing time. I quickly went into the bank and was greeted by some old friends. I cordially said hello to Mrs. Adolfson and walked over to Mr. Jacobs, the banker. He welcomed me back home and asked if I planned to stay around to help Mother with Father. Everyone in town knew of Father's condition. It was no secret. They all knew Father well and helped Mother when they could. After all, he was one of the reasons the town and area around the farms had prospered.

We spoke shortly about Father's condition and I finally explained why I was there to see him. I told him I had been working in Boston and had been paid a lot of money. We began to discuss what Father owed. I was surprised to learn it wasn't much. Mr. Jacobs told me that Father had always set aside a little extra money every time he came in to pay his debts. He told me with the little extra Father paid each month he was able to pay off the money borrowed to start the distillery and have some left to continue to save for Max and my college tuition.

I now told Mr. Jacobs how much I needed to deposit and once he heard the amount he gave me a wink. At first I didn't understand what it meant but later I learned he knew I was running whiskey to the States. He really didn't care where the money came from or how it was earned as long as I put it in his bank.

I made him agree that no one would learn of my savings and that, if Mother ever came to him to borrow any money or had any debt with the local merchants, he would see to it that my money would be used for settling any family debt. He agreed and also promised that if I ever needed money while I was away, he would make all arrangements with any bank in any town I was in to assist me when I needed it.

Mr. Jacobs and I became very good friends after that day. He helped me on many occasions. As independent as I was and with all the money I had deposited into his bank, I never realized I would ever need his help. Little did I know at that time how much Mr. Jacobs would become a very useful resource in the future? It was almost a blessing in disguise that we made the arrangement that we did.

We agreed no one would know what I was doing or how much money I was earning. Whatever money I used to purchase liquor from my parents I would have Mr. Jacobs deposit it into their business account.

Once I finalized the arrangement with Mr. Jacobs and secured my parents' debt, I got back to my business. Gus and I had less than two weeks to check out the *Black Duck*, repair any damage and reload the larger liquor cargo for the next trip. First we needed to remove the crate with the spare Liberty engine from the *Black Duck* and haul it back to the barn at the house.

I wasn't sure when we would have a chance to replace the old airplane Liberty but I felt we should do it as soon as possible so we wouldn't have to worry about being stranded in the Atlantic with illegal cargo.

Chapter Eleven

I brought Father down to the docks to see the old boat I purchased from his friend Captain John. I hoped it would spark some kind of memories in him of his friend. We picked up Gus on the way to the shore and Father remembered Gus. Gus had a distinct look and personality, one you could always recognize. Father knew Gus like he was his own son. I always admired my father for treating Gus like one of his children and with respect.

Gus's dad, Byron, showed my father how to build and repair everything we used to run the businesses. Father owed Byron a wealth of gratitude and he always showed it. Father was always stern with his employees but treated Gus's entire family as if they were relatives.

We finally made it down to the docks and when Father saw the *Black Duck* a big smile came over his face. Father didn't believe we were going for a ride on it. I showed him how Gus and I took the old engine we retrieved from the airplane many years earlier. He said he thought it was still in the shed after all these years. He said there were many days while I was gone that he thought about going out to the shed to try and get it running but never did.

We untied the dingy from the pier and rowed out to the boat. Once on board we pulled back the tarp and brought Father below to see the Liberty. We had taken on lots of water on our trip back from Boston so I started the boat and turned on the bilge pumps.

Father took a closer look at the engine and asked what the blower on it was used for. I told him it was a turbo-supercharger. It was driven by the engine exhaust and compressed air so more air could be forced into the intake manifold. The engine without it could only take in as much air as the vacuum from the downward pull of each cylinder would allow at the atmospheric pressure.

I also explained to Father that at higher elevations the air is thinner so the Liberty was fitted with the turbo-supercharger to maintain equal air intake and horsepower to fly the plane at higher altitudes. At sea level, in the *Black Duck*, it forced higher volumes of air to the point that horsepower was increased by at least thirty percent.

Father was amazed at how a simple internal combustion engine could be modified with a fan or blower to transform it from about three hundred and sixty horsepower to around four hundred and fifty horsepower. There was a price to pay for that extra power though. Although we needed it to haul the whiskey and still have extra power to elude anyone trying to catch us, it consumed much more fuel.

I explained to Father that I had to design the fuel tank to achieve a capacity where the horsepower to overall weight ratio matched. This way we were never without power when we needed it. Father continued to examine the Liberty as it ran. He adjusted the carburetor but it let out a big cloud of black smoke. He returned the carburetor setting to the correct position again and once more the Liberty ran as smooth as it was designed to.

Father and I went back up to the pilothouse while Gus pulled up the anchor. The Liberty was warmed up now and we were ready to go. I swung the boat around real quick and then came that smile again.

Not only did Gus and I have the smile on our faces but Father did also. We pulled out of the harbor at low throttle and once past the break wall, I started to increase the throttle.

The Liberty pushed us through the water like we were floating on air. The bow began to rise and the speed picked up more and more until the turbo-supercharger kicked in. I, to this day, am still impressed at how that old, beat up engine from the crashed airplane had found a new use with the help of Gus and myself by simply installing it into the old boat.

It was nice to play in the *Black Duck* without extra weight from liquor bottles but the next load to Boston would be our heaviest. Father still wasn't aware why we had the *Black Duck*. He thought we just used it to play around with or go fishing. If he ever found out we were running whiskey I didn't know what he would have done to us. I had to make sure no one would tell him. As long as I could keep Father away from the distillery we could get the whiskey we needed for the next trip.

I decided to move only a few cases of whiskey at a time to the *Black Duck* to be less conspicuous. I had Byron help us by taking Father into town once in a while. We arranged late mornings to move the liquor because that's when activity at the distillery was the highest. Everyone would be so busy they wouldn't have time to concern themselves with what I was doing.

Gus spent most of his time maintaining the *Black Duck*. A fifty-foot wooden boat always needed some type of repair and attention. If it wasn't for the fact we were making lots of money from the use of the boat it wouldn't have been worth keeping. That's the reason why Captain John wanted to scuttle it.

While Gus made the last few repairs on the *Black Duck* I used the time to spend with Father. It was nice being able to be with Father for the week and it gave Mother a little bit of extra time to do some of the things she needed to get done before Gus and I left again.

I suspected Mother had an idea what I was doing going back and forth to Boston and I finally worked up the courage to tell her. I wanted her to understand this was not going to continue very much longer because I had already saved enough money to make sure the businesses and the household had enough funds to manage for at least a few more years. I also told her about my meeting with Mr. Jacobs and asked her if she would meet with Father's lawyer to switch all the assets into her name or Max's.

I started to become worried that if something happened to me or Father, Mother and Max would have difficulties getting access to my money if they needed it to keep the businesses going. I knew deep inside that there was a very real possibility I could be caught by the Coast Guard and I would be sent to prison for transporting the illegal alcohol.

I also was afraid that if I did get caught I would be made an example of by the US Government and everything my parents had worked for may be lost trying to defend me. I'm sure Mother thought of the dangers also but we didn't discuss it in too much depth. She was somewhat disappointed in me but knew what I was doing was for the benefit of the entire family and all the people who worked for Father. She also liked the fact that I would be available to be with Father before he totally lost his recognition of us.

All the liquor had now been loaded and we still had almost a full week to transport it back to Boston. I decided to wait a few more days so I stayed around the house with Mother and Father just to be with them. I was starting to miss Max and made a mental note to visit him when I returned to Boston. School would be ending in a few months for the summer recess and I wondered if Max had made plans to stay in Boston or return to Blacks Harbour to relax during that time.

Knowing Max, I was sure he would do one of two things. Either he would continue to study in Boston during the time off so he could get ahead, or he would return home to help out in the business. I didn't want Max home, because once he discovered how bad Father was he may not return to school. That scenario would almost make it impossible for me to bring any more whiskey back to Boston. Max would stop it immediately.

I was being a little selfish with what I wanted. I did wonder for a moment if I should tell Max of Father's condition. As much as I cared for Father's health, I knew Max would be just as concerned. Max was much more logical than I though. He would want to find the best doctors and specialists to help Father, and I, on the other hand, would prefer Father enjoy the time he had the way he would want it, without doctors and specialists prodding and poking him with all types of tests.

I thought Father's condition was not an illness but a progression of age. We would all end up in the same place at some time in the future but we would all be there at different stages in our lives. Everyone born on earth, including Mother, Max, and me, would all be the same as Father when we became old. The only question there would be was at what age in our life would it occur?

After understanding we would all be in a similar situation as Father I realized it was something we had no control over. Maybe it was hereditary, maybe it was our diet or where we lived, or maybe it was just the way God planned it to be. But since there was nothing we could do about it there was no sense in worrying about it. My only hope was I could live my life to the fullest, spend as much time with Father as I could and accomplish as many of my dreams as possible before any type of disability occurred.

With all the banking concerns resolved and the arrangements finalized with Mr. Jacobs, everything I wanted to take care of while at home during this visit was complete. Mother was making plans to meet with Father's lawyer so I felt as though I could now leave for a week or so to get the next load of whiskey down to Boston.

Mother made dinner for Gus and me at the farmhouse and invited Gus's mother and father to join us. We all had such a great time that evening. Father and Byron told stories of how they met and of the adventures they had together. Even though the Civil War had ended in the late eighteen eighties and Negroes were supposed to be free, Father had to pretend Byron belonged to him so no one would bother him.

Father wasn't the one telling the stories though, it was Byron. Father was having difficulty recalling all the details. Mother and Gus's mom would add their version from time to time. I think Mother would embellish a little to create some excitement in the stories. Mother was a great storyteller and I think some of it has worn off on me.

After listening for a while I began to understand why Byron was so devoted to Father. Father had taken care of him and now the role was starting to reverse. Soon Byron would be taking care of Father. I wondered if the same would occur with Gus and me. Would Gus be the one to take care of me as I grew to an old man?

Chapter Twelve

The *Black Duck* was loaded with fuel, liquor and the supplies we needed for the next few days. I asked Byron to drive us down to the dock so he could bring the truck back to the farm after we left. The morning air was crisp and cold, the water was still and the tide was high. Once we pulled out of the harbor I realized the extra weight was taxing the Liberty more than previously.

I began to wonder if we were going to make it to Boston on time. We still had a few days and if I calculated correctly we would have plenty of time to make the delivery. As usual, the trip started out as planned. We followed our regular course out to open waters and beyond the twelve-mile limit. We followed the coast and kept our eyes open for the Coast Guard or other boaters.

I preferred not to encounter anyone so we could keep the trips as quiet as possible. We didn't need to let anyone know we were out there just in case the Coast Guard had private boaters reporting back to them. In this business we couldn't trust anyone.

I hadn't heard from Kieran or Shamus before we left Blacks Harbour but I knew they would be waiting for us when we arrived. I remember them giving me strict orders to be back in exactly two weeks and nothing else needed to be said.

Gus and I settled into our favorite spots on the boat now that we were on our way. I preferred the pilothouse and Gus liked being on deck. He enjoyed looking out all around us to see if anyone was out there. Other than a few seagulls he mostly just stared out at open waters.

I began to learn the charts much better, to the point where I didn't need to look out, just maintain my speed, read the compass and follow the charts. Captain John would be proud of me. He taught me so much about how to prepare and travel the open waters that I could never repay him. Many of the people I had met in the last year helped me to grow and changed my life dramatically. I was very fortunate to have so many good friends around me.

Gus and I continued on our planned course. Gus watched out as I steered the boat. After a few hours of nothing I began to doze off. I kept catching my head tipping forward as I became more tired. It had only been a few hours into the journey since we left Blacks Harbour and we still had quite a bit of ocean to cover before we would reach our destination. I decided to get some food in me to help keep focused.

We ate a few sandwiches Mother gave us and downed it with black coffee. The black coffee tasted so good. I rarely drank it because it gave me the shakes. As it was, I had such a high level of energy that coffee usually put me over the top. Gus could drink it for hours and it never bothered him.

After eating I let Gus steer the *Black Duck* so I could take a rest. It was my turn to sit on deck and breathe in the fresh sea air and watch the open ocean for a while. During my watch I began to daydream about the future. I imagined Shannon and myself being together as we grew older. I didn't see a house, farm or anything else young couples think of or long for. I thought it to be strange I didn't see any of that. Usually my thoughts of the future were very vivid to me.

I guess I was too tired to focus on seeing our future together. I started to think about all the homeless children I had seen in Boston and wondered how many of them there really were or how many there must have been around the entire United States. I began to think I needed to develop some kind of plan to help these children. I knew Shannon would never interfere with me doing something good and I was sure she would be as passionate as I to help.

I thought I would see Joe while in Boston this trip and wanted to ask him to help me find an abandoned building or warehouse. I could convert it to a place for the homeless children to be safe and have a warm place to sleep. I made more money than I needed and I wanted to do something good with the proceeds from the illegal liquor runs. I knew I could keep all the money for myself and Shannon but something inside continued to tell me to do something good with the money and to help the homeless children.

I started to doze off while daydreaming so I went to the pilothouse to tell Gus I was going to rest below deck for a little while. I asked him not to repeat the same episode as the last trip and get us lost again. I think he learned his lesson the last time and would never fall asleep again while in charge.

I went below deck and rested for a few hours. When I returned topside it was dark and Gus had kept his word not to fall asleep. I went to get some coffee and realized Gus had finished it. I guess it was the only way he could stay awake while I slept.

I washed up to refresh myself and made some more coffee. I urged Gus to go below and get some rest for himself. I needed him to help offload the whiskey when we reached Boston, because Kieran or Shamus never wanted to help us. He agreed and went below for his turn.

I enjoyed the nighttime while traveling on the water. As long as we kept the lights off and our distance from shore no one would ever know we were out there. As the clouds rolled in and it grew darker I began to rely more on the compass and charts. Gus just read the compass while steering and I would only let him steer during daylight hours. At some point I would need to teach Gus how to read the charts; in case something happened to me he would still be able to navigate home.

As we grew closer and closer to Boston I thought more of being with Shannon. She was in my heart everywhere I went. I missed her every time we were apart. I began to get excited thinking about telling her my plans for the homeless children and finding a place for them to live. I was always at ease with myself whenever I was with her or thinking of her.

I went below to see if Gus had fallen asleep. He was out like a dog napping on a porch on a hot summer day. It started getting a little chilly so I found a blanket and covered Gus. As I returned up to the pilothouse I could hear another engine running in the distance. It sounded like a diesel so I wrote it off as a fishing boat heading out to sea.

The sound slowly grew closer and closer as if it were coming straight towards us. I couldn't see them so I knew they couldn't see us. As the sound came closer I reduced our throttle to an idle so as to hide the Liberty's powerful, smooth-running murmur. I needed to know what direction the other boat was coming from in order to avoid it. I was tempted to turn on our lights only to get the direction and just as I thought it, a big spotlight shone down onto the *Black Duck* from over our bow.

The light scared the hell out of me and blinded me for a moment. I couldn't have imagined who was out there in the black of the night with no lights on. Why would they want anything from us unless they wanted to steal our cargo and sink the boat?

We carried no weapons so if someone did try to take the *Black Duck* and the cargo we couldn't defend ourselves other than try to outrun them. At first I thought it was another runner looking to see who we were but that wouldn't be normal. They would have stayed quiet and motionless like us. Maybe it was just a fishing vessel trying to avoid us because they heard our engine but couldn't see us.

All of a sudden I heard shouting from a bullhorn and several other lights were shining down on us. Being blinded by the lights and hearing the loud noise made me confused and disoriented. It became clear to me it had to be the Coast Guard and they were heading straight for us. I thought they were going to ram us and sink us.

Using that tactic they would be getting another rum runner off the water and no one but themselves would know what had happened. No one who knew us would call us in missing if we didn't show up in Boston or Blacks Harbour.

I quickly swung the *Black Duck* around and gave the engine more throttle. It was clearly too late, the cutter had built up enough speed and we had too much weight from carrying the heavier load of whiskey to get away. All kinds of thoughts started running through my head. I thought it shouldn't end this way. I wanted a life to live. I wanted to be with Shannon. I wanted to help all the homeless children. This couldn't be happening to me. This wasn't supposed to happen.

I felt this was it, Gus and I were caught and he was still below deck asleep. He had no idea what was going on and I would have to wake him to tell him we were going to prison and the boat and cargo would be confiscated.

I had never felt so helpless in my life. Gus had come with me not knowing the dangers and I put him in this situation. Our parents were going to be furious with me and it wouldn't matter because I would be in jail. Maybe they would let Gus go home if I told them he had no idea what we were carrying. That wouldn't work. They would find out eventually that he knew everything and we would both end up rotting in prison.

I couldn't go to prison. I couldn't do this to Gus. He had lived a sheltered life and now he wouldn't even be able to go home or do anything else in his life. Adrenaline started pumping through my heart and body from all the drama and excitement. My mind and body weren't mine anymore. Something came over me and it took over all my senses.

My body went into a self-running mode. I really had no control. It was like intuition was leading me. I decided I would give it a last try to get away. What did we have to lose? The way I saw it there was no other way out. It was either try something or give up and go to prison or, even worse, get killed. I was not one to give up and go down without a fight.

I remember Father had adjusted the fuel mixture that caused the large cloud of black smoke to appear. It was easy to do from the pilothouse because I had earlier rigged up the lever to adjust the fuel flow depending on how the Liberty ran. I pushed the lever all the way down and it worked just as I had hoped it would.

With the moonless, cloud-covered dark of the night and the large screen of black smoke, even the powerful beam from the cutter's light couldn't penetrate it. What a great feeling it was thinking we actually may have a slight chance to get away. I turned the *Black Duck* to the right then back to the left.

Since the Coast Guardsmen couldn't see us anymore I wanted the maneuver to confuse them as to which direction we were going since they could still hear the roar of the Liberty engine. I just wanted to create a little more space between us.

I still couldn't get up enough speed to get away so I began to pray for some kind of miracle. I had no clue if we were going to get away or what was going to happen but I still kept praying. As I turned around I could see the cutter's light fading even though the black smoke screen started to lift. My adrenaline was still pumping and my heart was racing faster and faster. It looked like we were going to get away. I was overwhelmed and in shock when I saw what was really happening.

As the black smoke faded totally away there was a spooky fog all around us and a single, twinkling light was shining in the distance behind our boat. It wasn't the cutter's light because it was too dim. I looked around and shouted to see if it was another boat. We had just managed to get away from the Coast Guard cutter and I thought maybe there were others out there also. No way would we be able to escape if there was another one.

To my surprise the miracle I prayed for turned out to be the ghost ship the *Isidore*. This time I was glad to see the *Isidore*. It passed between the cutter and the *Black Duck*. This time I was sure someone besides me had to see it. If it stopped the Coast Guard from continuing to follow us I knew for sure they had seen it also. My heart was still racing from the excitement and a state of panic overwhelmed me. How could the *Isidore* just appear out of nowhere?

I shouldn't have been so surprised; after all, it did happen once before but this time it was there to help. I began to refocus on getting as far out from shore as possible so we would be out of reach of the Coast Guard. I thought for a moment, Gus and I had just come so close to going to jail but as luck would have it we got away.

I wondered if the *Isidore* was just a figment of my imagination and if maybe something had happened to the cutter mechanically that caused it to stop. I couldn't fully believe that it had appeared to help me or that it really had appeared at all. Whatever happened, I will never fully understand. I never told anyone what happened that day, not Gus or even Shannon. I kept the secret to myself because I thought no one would ever believe it.

I finally relaxed after speeding away as far as I could. I needed to check the charts and compass to make sure I was traveling east and not back into shore. I was going out to sea and away from the Coast Guard. Everything I wanted to happen came true, the screen of black smoke and the miracle I had prayed for. Once again, God was watching over me. Why should I be so lucky? Was there some other, bigger reason God wanted me safe?

Gus finally came topside and had no clue what had just happened. He awoke from the commotion of the *Black Duck* being jostled around and thought it was just from rough seas or bad weather. I didn't mention a word to him. I thought the less he knew the better off he would be if we ever did get caught and he was interrogated.

I calmed down and began to think, was it really the *Isidore*, and why did it show up when it did? I was happy to see it though. This time I was not afraid of it and realized, for some reason, something had attracted it to us. Why, I would never know. I told Gus I wanted a drink of whiskey and told him to go below and bring up a bottle. We never drank alcohol before other than to taste the quality we produced in the distillery, and then, once in a while. Gus looked at me strangely and retrieved the bottle.

After each of us took a swig from the bottle he asked what the occasion was. I told him summer would be coming soon and Max would probably be returning home. If he did, we wouldn't be able to continue our adventures, so I toasted to a safe trip to Boston and back home without any incidences or being caught. We cheered a second toast to seeing the girls again soon.

I knew deep inside this wouldn't be our last trip. It had become too thrilling for me to give it all up. Anyway, soon Prohibition had to end and we could get back to running the business and transporting the liquor to the United States as Father had originally planned—legally. I needed to figure out a way to make the next few trips safer. I didn't want to get caught and the episode I just encountered was too close for comfort.

I was worried if I told Shamus and Kieran what happened out at sea they wouldn't buy liquor from us anymore. Kieran did tell me, before I brought down the first load, that if I ever did get caught he wouldn't be able to help us. We would be on our own. I had to figure a way to get away from the Coast Guard or anyone else chasing us whenever we were running full loads.

Chapter Thirteen

Cautiously, as the sun began to rise out of the ocean behind us, we slowly approached the coast. We met up with Shamus and Kieran in our usual place near Rockport. They were there exactly in the same spot at the same time we arrived. Gus and I offloaded the liquor and then helped the truck driver and his helper move everything up the shore and into the waiting trucks.

As the trucks drove off, Kieran handed me my money. Now with the *Black Duck* empty, we didn't need to worry about the Coast Guard. We sat on shore and counted the money. I found it was short five thousand dollars. I called back to Kieran and asked why he shorted us. He looked at me angrily and said, "I told you to call Shannon before you left Canada and you didn't do what I told you. Every time we make plans you have to follow them or it will cost you. If you don't like it, too bad, listen to what I tell you next time and there won't be any issues. Besides, you still owed me for the Liberty engine you took the last time you were here. Did you forget about that?"

Kieran had taken twenty five hundred for the Liberty since I picked the one with the turbo-supercharger. The other twenty five hundred was the penalty for not following instructions. Shamus said, "The next time you don't do what we say we'll take more." I was still angry with them but knew if they really wanted to they didn't have to give me anything. There was nothing I could do about it other than not bring down any more liquor.

I learned many valuable lessons that day. One was, even when dealing with illegal businessmen it was still business and I had to keep my word once I agreed. If you can't deliver, don't say you can.

I stashed the money, started the *Black Duck*, pulled up the anchor and headed straight down to Boston. I needed to refuel and to find Shannon. At this point I just wanted to be with her and hold her in my arms. Even Gus was looking forward to seeing Carol again. I'm not sure how he really felt about her and it wasn't my business to ask anyway but all I could think about was being with Shannon again.

We each had our own reasons for being with the girls and mine started to be more than just companionship or affection. I wanted to be more to Shannon than just a guy she met from Canada. I wanted her to be with me for the rest of my life. I planned to head over to the restaurant once we docked the boat. I asked Gus to stay on the *Black Duck* and I promised I would return shortly. He knew one of us had to watch the boat so he agreed to stay and went below to make himself something to eat.

When I walked through town it felt good to be back in Boston. When I arrived at the restaurant not only was Shannon waiting for me but Joe was there also. I didn't know why he was there. Maybe Kieran told him I complained about the money he had taken. I didn't want to bring up the subject. I didn't want another lecture. I thought it may be a perfect time to ask about a warehouse. Joe asked me to come downstairs and told me to sit down.

Joe said he was starting to worry about me. He said he heard about the incident with the Coast Guard the evening before and wanted to know what I was going to do to not let it happen again. I explained it had been an unfortunate circumstance and I would be more careful the next time. I wondered how he knew. I didn't say anything to anyone about the night before, not even Gus, and he was on the boat. Something wasn't right. There was more about Joe than I knew, and to be honest, I really didn't want to get too deep into his affairs.

As we continued to talk he said he wanted some assurance because if I were caught it would have a drastic effect on his business. I asked him how he knew what had happened and he said, "In this town, I know everything that happens." Him telling me that made me feel very uncomfortable. How could he know everything about the Coast Guard and so quickly? After all, he was the one buying the illegal liquor. If he was connected to the Coast Guard, why wouldn't he just tell them to leave me alone?

Once that discussion was over, Joe knew I would hold up my end of the deals from now on and not disappoint him. I asked Joe if he could help me find a warehouse to buy. Curiously, he asked me what I wanted to do with a warehouse in Boston. Joe probably thought I was going to bring loads for other restaurants and needed a place to store it.

I could see Joe didn't want anyone else to have liquor so he could be the only one selling it in Boston. I told Joe I wanted to set up a shelter for the homeless children in the city. I had enough money to take care of myself, my family and Shannon, if she wanted me to, for the rest of our lives. What extra money I made I would put aside for others. This way I wouldn't feel guilty about what I was doing.

I said I wanted to do more with my life than just run liquor. I wanted to help others who needed it more than me. At first he thought I was crazy to help people I didn't even know but he realized by the look in my eyes I was serious about what I was telling him.

Joe asked me if I had ever lied in my life and I immediately told him no. By the way I answered so quickly he knew I was telling him the truth. He told me to go back to the boat and he would have Kieran get back to me with an answer. I asked him if it would be okay to spend a little time with Shannon and my brother Max before I returned to the boat and he agreed.

We went back upstairs from the bar in the basement to the restaurant. Just before Joe walked away he said he would do what he could to help me achieve my dreams. Shannon looked at us and probably wondered what he had meant when he said that.

Once Joe was gone my full attention turned to Shannon again. I had asked if Carol was around and Shannon told me it was her day off. She was upstairs getting ready to see Gus again. Carol overheard Kieran and Shamus discussing we were back. Shannon asked if it were all right for Carol to go to the boat while I stayed with her. I didn't hesitate to say it was okay.

Shannon asked me to go wash up and she would make me lunch. While I was cleaning up Carol came downstairs. As I walked back to the counter Shannon was whispering something into Carol's ear. Both girls giggled and Carol waved good-bye to me as she left to go see Gus. Shannon was setting up a place at the counter for me to sit and eat.

The restaurant was quiet that day. It made it easy for Shannon to spend a little time with me while I ate. It was almost as if it was planned that way. A few patrons had finished eating, placed their money on the tables and left. The next thing I knew we were all alone. Shannon, with her elbows on the counter and her closed fists under her chin, stared into my eyes as I ate my food. She said she had missed me more than I would ever know. I was thinking the same about her as she spoke the words to me.

It was so strange. It was as if she knew what I was thinking. I wondered if she wanted me as much as I wanted her. If I wanted to know for sure I would have to build up the courage and ask her. It was time to know. It was also time to tell her about my dreams of being with her for the rest of my life.

My head was spinning wildly with all that had happened to me over the last twenty-four hours. Due to the episode with the Coast Guard and the *Isidore* showing up again, Kieran shorting me money because I didn't call before I left, Joe being at the restaurant to talk to me, and now the thought of telling Shannon I wanted to be with her forever, my mind and body were exhausted emotionally and physically.

I tried to find the words to tell her but they wouldn't come to me. I realized it may not have been the right time so I let fate take its course. When the time was right it would happen; there was no need to force the issue. Besides, I was tired and really wasn't thinking straight.

Shannon asked if I would see her again that evening and as far as I was concerned I wasn't going anywhere for the rest of the day. My intention was to stay at the restaurant until it closed since Carol and Gus would be at the boat. Shannon asked that I leave for a while to give her a chance to clean up. Since it was Carol's day off she would need to take care of everything in order to close up. The cook would only take care of making meals and it was up to the rest of the help to do all the other work.

I wanted to check back with Gus to make sure he was okay. I also needed to see Max. It had been awhile since I had spoken to him and I wanted to find out what he was planning for the summer. I told Shannon I had a few things to do and that I would stop back later. She asked me to come back after six o'clock and we could go for a walk around the city. I kissed her on the cheek and said I'd be back.

She smiled at me as I pushed my empty plate towards her. It was the kind of smile that seemed mischievous. I wondered what Shannon had on her mind. I wondered if it had something to do with her and Carol whispering to each other earlier.

I left to go find Max at the campus but had no idea where he would be. He could have been anywhere. Once I reached the school I decided to go straight to his dorm room. I didn't expect to find him there but hoped someone would know if he were in class, at the library, or at a study hall.

Someone other than Max answered the door. I had never met the boy before but then again I hadn't spent any time with Max at the dorm. I introduced myself as Max's younger brother and he told me his name was Hiram. I had no idea Max was sharing a room but knowing Max was always careful as to how he spent money, sharing the room was cheaper than living alone.

Hiram said Max was at class but he expected him back any minute now. He invited me in to wait if I wanted to. I really had no place else to go so I went in and sat down. Hiram said he had just moved in with Max. They had recently met in a study hall and had much in common. He said they had both complained about their first roommates and decided if they could they would try to change and share a room. Both had helped their parents with businesses before coming to school. Hiram's family was also in the liquor business.

Now I knew why they had much in common. In just a short conversation I realized these two boys, Max and Hiram, would be friends for a long time. Max had walked in the door and gave me an embrace as I stood up. It was so nice to feel Max's warmth as he hugged me. It reminded me of when we were kids and Mother would come into our rooms at night to hug us before we went to bed.

Mother taught us there is no shame in brothers hugging or men hugging. I always thought it to be special that Max and I had no inhibitions about showing our affection for each other, even in public.

Hiram smiled and said it was his tradition to share a meal with a good friend's relative when they met for the first time. I reluctantly had to decline because I was meeting Shannon for dinner. I apologized and explained the circumstances. Hiram said he understood, especially if a lady was the reason I couldn't oblige.

Max and I went for a walk to talk in private for a while. I asked him if he had heard from Mother or Father lately and he said he had recently spoken to Mother. I didn't know the two of them stayed in touch. Max told me he was aware of Father's condition and thanked me for not telling him earlier.

Max said if he had known earlier he would have left school to take care of Father but Mother talked him out of it. Mother told Max that I had been back home a few times and that I had given her back the money she saved for me to attend college. Max asked if I had any plans to continue school later but I told him I wasn't sure what I was going to do.

I explained to Max that for now I would keep working for Albert Hoffman at the gasoline filling station when in town and would continue bringing supplies back and forth between home and Boston when there was a need. Mother told Max that I bought Captain John's old boat and fixed it up. She also told him I finally got the old airplane engine out of the shed and actually got it running.

Max said Mother was proud of me for finding a use for the old engine and that I was doing something productive with my time. Mother also told Max a few other things that weren't the truth, but Max didn't really need to know what I was doing with the boat.

Mother told Max I was helping Captain John transport goods when he had extra work and couldn't handle the loads himself. She said he was doing it to keep me out of trouble and to help bring in a little extra money because Father was ill. I told him, other than fuel for the boat and money for supplies and Gus's pay, everything else I earned from Captain John went back to Mother to help with the house expenses.

I just remembered, as I mentioned Gus's name, that I had to get back to the boat. I was so much enjoying catching up with Max that I had lost all track of time. I realized Mother set the stage for Max and me to get closer together. Since we were both becoming men she knew it was time for us to start acting like men. I could never thank her enough for not saying anything to Max about what I was really doing.

I told Max that I would come back in a few days but had to get back to Gus and the boat to make sure everything was okay. I shook his hand and thanked him for giving me so much of his time. I asked him to let Hiram know I would be back to take up his offer for dinner at another time. Max said he would let him know and looked forward to it.

Chapter Fourteen

I realized it had become very risky to come into town in the *Black Duck* even if I wasn't carrying liquor. I hid the boat down the Mystic River this trip in order to conceal it from the Coast Guard. Although it was a longer walk to Harvard and the North End from the Mystic River it was definitely safer. After the last run-in with the Coast Guard I knew they would start looking for the *Black Duck* more vigorously from now on.

The Coast Guard station was at the mouth of the Charles River and it would have been much easier to get to Harvard and other locations if I could get down the Charles River. After this trip we would have to leave the boat further north. I couldn't continue taking the risk of leaving Gus alone to be responsible to watch over the *Black Duck*.

It wasn't fair for me to leave Gus at the boat all the time either. If the Coast Guard did find him alone they would easily intimidate him.

From now on I would have to hide the *Black Duck* offshore in the tall reeds near Rockport and travel the rest of the way by land. I would need to buy an automobile and leave it where I could retrieve it in order to get back and forth between Boston and Rockport.

As I walked from the Harvard campus back to the *Black Duck* I noticed that there were big beautiful Victorian homes along the way. Some of the wealthiest and most influential families of Boston were settled in this part of town. These were probably some of the people buying the good liquor I was bringing down from Canada. With the money I was making I really didn't care who was buying the liquor.

I finally reached the *Black Duck* and found Carol and Gus sitting on deck enjoying the night air. They didn't know I was watching them from a short distance but I could see they were all wrapped up in each other and didn't worry who was watching. I had originally planned to stop by for a little while but since everything was fine, there was no need for me to interrupt.

It started to get late and I needed to get back to the restaurant to see Shannon. By now Shannon was probably wondering what was taking me so long. I walked past the *Black Duck* and headed to the North End. I still had quite a bit of distance to cover and it was getting late.

Over the next few miles, as I got closer to the restaurant, I saw more and more homeless children on the streets. It was still hard for me to believe with all the wealth in this town no one was trying to help them.

When I arrived at the restaurant all the lights were off and the street was dark. It was a little odd that the lights were out but when I reached the front door there was a note tacked to it. It was from Shannon. She asked me to walk around the corner to the alley. There would be a set of stairs to get to the second floor above the restaurant.

I was a little nervous because I was late, and I had never been in Shannon's apartment before. I found the alley and walked up the stairs. I knocked on the door and Shannon immediately opened the door and greeted me. My heart began to pound as I watched her excitement in seeing me. She reached out and gave me a big hug. She said she was very worried about me and asked what had taken so long.

We walked inside and stopped in the parlor. I sat in a big cozy lounge chair and explained a little about the time I spent with Max and Hiram. She could see I was exhausted and knelt down to the floor beside me. She slipped off my shoes, lifted my feet and slid an ottoman underneath them. With my legs resting and my body sunk into the chair I could have easily fallen asleep.

Shannon made dinner for the two of us since Carol and Gus were at the boat. She called me into the dining area after she lit some candles. She had gone out of her way to make the evening romantic, which made me feel guilty for arriving so late. I was still a little nervous knowing we were finally together with no one else around.

During dinner I told Shannon about my father and his health. She asked if I planned to return home and stay to take care of him. Shannon began to ask questions about us, about my plans for the future and what I planned to do after Prohibition ended. She looked worried and I couldn't understand why. I had no intention of changing anything.

We discussed my plans to buy a building from Joe to start the homeless shelter for the children on the streets. I had saved enough money and all we needed was some support from the local merchants and churches. Shannon said she was willing to help but wanted to get back to the subject of us. I could see she really cared for me and wanted more than just a visit every time I returned. It was no secret, there were lots of eligible men courting her, but it seemed she always waited to be with me.

Shannon said she had been thinking about the two of us being together more often. She said she had worked at the restaurant for a while now and had some time off coming to her. She was thinking of taking a trip to New York to visit her parents, sister and younger brother. She said she wanted to bring me along to meet them.

I started to see where the conversation was going. I told Shannon I had plans for us also and that we needed to discuss it more when I was rested. I hadn't slept in a while and needed to have a clear head. We both walked into the parlor and I sat back into the lounge chair. Shannon turned on a radio and played some soft music. Once again Shannon sat at my side on the floor and rested her head on my knees.

With her head on my lap I gently stroked her beautiful hair. While talking I leaned my head back into the chair and fell into a deep sleep. I could still hear Shannon talking to me even although I had dozed off. She had lots of plans for us to be together and I remember dreaming she kissed me on my forehead and covering me with a blanket.

I woke up the next morning and found the apartment empty. I assumed Shannon had gone downstairs to work but wasn't sure. A short while later Carol showed up. Carol said she had asked Shannon to cover her shift that morning while she was with Gus. Carol also said she would change and go to relieve Shannon so the two of us could spend the day together.

After Carol left I washed up so I could be ready when Shannon returned. I wanted Shannon to come with me to Joe's bank across the street so we could make arrangements to buy a warehouse. I wanted Shannon to know I truly cared for her and that I wanted to be with her for the rest of my life.

When Shannon returned we sat at the kitchen table and talked about starting the homeless shelter. I asked her for some paper and began to write what would be needed. I asked her if I did purchase a building from Joe could she really find others to help. Shannon looked a little perplexed. She asked where I found all the energy considering how tired I was the evening before.

Shannon knew how much it meant to me to help the homeless children. I had spoken about it so many times and now I had the ability to make it a reality. She knew once I started I would make it happen but I couldn't do it alone. I needed her help and the help of her friends. She said she wanted to be with me also but had an agreement with the restaurant to continue working there. She said when her parents left for New York they needed to borrow some money. Joe provided the funds and it was her obligation to work at the restaurant until the debt was paid. I told Shannon not to worry and that I would pay what was left she owed.

Shannon changed out of her work clothes and walked across the street with me to the bank. Joe's secretary, Elizabeth, gave us some addresses with properties that had been foreclosed. Elizabeth said Joe told her I would be coming in soon to ask about buildings so she prepared the information in advance. We looked over the papers and asked if we could see some of the buildings. Elizabeth said she would call Shamus to take us around.

When Shamus arrived Joe was with him. Joe motioned for us to get into the automobile and we went for a little ride. Joe asked that we be careful what we do with the building because he suspected we were being watched. As long as the building was only used for housing the homeless children we would be left alone. If we decided to bring liquor down on our own and try to sell it to others besides him there would be repercussions.

Joe said he wanted to help me because I reminded him of himself when he was younger; ambitious and eager. I promised him I would only help the homeless children and nothing more. As far as the liquor I had no intentions of bringing it for anyone else but him and I hadn't planned on doing it for much longer. Plus, how much longer could Prohibition last?

We pulled back up to the bank and Joe stepped out. He once again reminded me to be careful and to watch my back. He said he had many eyes but couldn't watch after me everywhere I went. He also said if I did buy a building I should put it in someone else's name other than mine. If anything were to happen to me at least the property would be safe. I closed the door and just stared at him through the half open window. I wondered as Shamus drove off, did Joe really care for me as much as he said or was he just trying to keep me satisfied so I would continue to bring liquor from home?

Shamus, Shannon and I then drove around town the rest of the morning inspecting buildings. We finally came upon an old building that was clean and in pretty good condition. It had been used as a factory and had nice wood floors. The basement had a makeshift kitchen and lockers which I assumed were for the workers. The top three floors were wide open spaces. I walked around the second floor by myself while Shannon and Shamus stayed on the first floor.

I could hear them talking about how the kitchen equipment could be cleaned up and repaired. While listening to them my mind began to imagine the possibilities of converting the building to a home for the children. It seemed perfect for what I wanted to use it for.

After spending about fifteen minutes walking through the top floors I decided this was the building I would buy. When I returned downstairs to the basement Shannon had Shamus moving some of the kitchen equipment around to see whether it would fit her needs. I was happy to see she was feeling a part of the project, because after all, I couldn't do it without her.

Shamus had worked up a sweat moving the equipment around and had enough. I wondered why he helped her move the equipment when he never helped Gus and me move the liquor off the boat. I guessed Shannon and he were friends and he did it for her. We had spent enough time at the warehouse and we needed to get back. I still had to finalize the deal with the bank and get back to the *Black Duck* to see if Gus was all right.

When Shamus went to get the automobile Shannon and I stayed to lock up. We looked at each other and realized this was the building we were looking for but it still needed lots of work to make it a shelter for the street children. I could see in Shannon's eyes she was as excited as I was. She knew if we started the shelter together we would be together all the time.

Shamus pulled around to the front door and we hopped in the automobile. He looked at us and asked if we wanted to see any more buildings. At the exact same time, Shannon and I both said, "No." It was as if we were reading each other's minds again. I said to Shamus we found the building we were looking for and asked him to bring us back to the bank.

We drove back to the bank to finalize the deal with Elizabeth. I didn't care how much Joe wanted for the building, at that time my mind was only thinking about what I was planning to do with it. The price she told me was fair and I told her I would have the money transferred down from Canada later in the week. She said not to transfer any money and that I would need to talk to Kieran about payment. When I walked outside the bank Kieran and Shamus were waiting for me. Kieran told me I would need to bring three loads of liquor to cover the cost of the building. They didn't want any relationship between me and the bank. He also wanted to know whose name should be put on the deed after the loads were delivered. I told him I would let him know soon.

After the discussion about the payment arrangements I asked Shamus if he would take me over to see Albert. From there I could borrow Albert's truck to get back to Gus and the *Black Duck*. I felt bad for leaving Gus for such a long time but there were things I needed to take care of and I hoped he would understand.

I walked Shannon back to the restaurant and thanked her for all her help and encouragement. She said she wanted the children's shelter to become a reality as much as I wanted, and that she would be there for me when I needed her help. I kissed her gently on the lips and held her in my arms. The passion I had for her was growing even stronger and I began to feel she was falling in love with me also.

While driving to Albert's station I realized how much Shannon wanted to share my dreams with me. We could be happy together for a long time. If I could make a little more money bringing the liquor down we wouldn't have to worry. Once the next three loads were delivered I would own the building outright. Now I knew why Joe was so eager to help me with finding a warehouse. As long as I had the responsibility of keeping the children fed and sheltered I would need money. The only way I was making money was by selling the liquor to him. Starting the shelter assured Joe, at least for a little while, I would continue running the whiskey.

I knew there was a motive for Joe to help me. I really didn't care though. As long as he wanted liquor I could continue making the money I needed to keep the distillery back home out of trouble and the shelter would keep the children off the streets.

We reached Albert's filling station and I thanked Shamus for all his help. He fueled up his automobile, took a walk into the garage to check on some cargo he had stored there and left shortly after. After I helped Albert with a few customers we went inside to talk for a little while. He was very happy to see me and glad to see I was doing well.

Albert said he missed me and wondered when I would return to see him. I told him about the building I had just bought and that I needed his help. I explained that I had discussed with Joe putting the deed in someone else's name and asked if he wouldn't mind if I used his. Albert said he didn't mind but I would need to also put Shannon's or Max's name on the deed so he wouldn't be totally responsible for it.

I actually thought that was a better idea. If Shannon's name was also on the deed she would never have to worry about losing the building, because we could both trust Albert.

I asked Albert how much I could trust Joe. He told me there was one thing I needed to remember about Joe. As long as Joe was making money you could trust him. Joe was a businessman and buying the building was a business deal. I should look at it that way. He said if you take the personal feelings out of a business deal you will always make the right decisions.

I thought about what Albert told me for a long time. At first I didn't understand what he meant by saying I had to take the personal feelings out of the business deal but later it all became very clear. And he was right, Joe was a businessman and his objective was to make money.

Albert and I talked for a little while longer and I asked him if I could borrow the truck again. Albert said he had no need for it for a few days and told me I could return it when I was done with it.

I jumped in Albert's truck and headed out to the *Black Duck* to check on Gus and to see if everything was still all right. When I arrived I asked Gus to drive the truck to Rockport and I would bring the *Black Duck* up and meet him. Once there, we could find a place to leave it that would be safe so we could return to Boston.

Chapter Fifteen

In midsummer of nineteen hundred and twenty-seven everything was moving along as planned. Gus and I completed the three liquor runs needed to pay for the building in Boston and we did it quickly with no incident. It was a relief to have the three loads delivered because I didn't want the debt hanging over me. I didn't owe anyone anything and I wanted to keep it that way. Now with the liquor delivered I could hopefully spend some of the free time with Shannon.

Shannon decided not to go to New York but to have her sister Mary travel up to Boston. She arranged for Mary to work at the restaurant while she solicited local merchants and churches for donations to get the shelter started. I was surprised to find that merchants and churches were willing to give as much time, money and materials as they did. Shannon was able to set up the entire building with the support and donations she received.

Now with the property paid for and the donations covering most of the furnishings she could run it full time. There were even women from the churches who volunteered to cook and clean in order to give Shannon some free time for herself. Once the children on the street found out that the shelter was available for them to sleep in and where they could get a hot meal, they slowly started coming around.

The older boys were the first to come. They were grateful that someone had taken the time to do something for them. As it worked out, once the older boys saw everything was on the up and up they began to bring the younger boys around. Many of them hadn't had a decent meal or bath in weeks. In a way, Shannon was actually helping to lift the responsibility for the little guys off the older boys.

No pressure was put on any of the boys to stay at the shelter but if they did they would have to follow some simple rules and do some work to help out. There would need to be someone around all day and night to watch over the young ones. Shannon, her sister Mary, the older boys and the church ladies all took turns. Even Shamus and Kieran chipped in once in a while to make sure no trouble started with the older boys who came from different sections of town.

Albert hired one of the older boys from the shelter to work with him at the filling station. Once some of the other merchants saw that Albert had taken a chance with one of the boys, and it had worked out, they began to inquire of Shannon to see if any of the other boys were interested in helping them with their businesses. Everything started to fit together better than I had anticipated. Albert even started teaching some of the boys some basic mechanics and automotive engineering in the evenings at the filling station.

Not all the boys were receptive to us. There were many who had been abused, beaten, starved and who knows what else. These boys were finding it difficult to believe that not all adults were mean and abusive. These boys thought the shelter was a trap to get them off the streets or make them work for no money. I learned from these boys that you can't help anyone who doesn't want it.

Now with the shelter running well, I wanted to go home to visit my parents. I couldn't stop thinking how lucky I was to have parents who cared for me and that I had a place to call home. I spoke to Shannon about coming with Gus and me to Blacks Harbour but she said she thought it would be better if she stayed in Boston. She wanted to spend some time with her sister and keep an eye on the boys to make sure everyone was taken care of. I couldn't get over her dedication to the shelter, especially since it was my idea and not hers.

I bought the old truck from Albert and had the boy whom Albert hired come with Gus and me to Rockport. We went to the *Black Duck* so we could go home. I instructed the boy to bring the truck back to Albert's filling station and told the boy if Shannon needed the truck for hauling furniture or supplies he could take it to help her. The boy agreed and promised only to use the truck to help at the shelter.

Gus and I picked up a few supplies before heading back to Canada. The weather started to change for the worse. Thunderclouds rolled in and the rain came down hard. We quickly checked the boat over and decided to head out to open water. I hoped we could outrun the storm and once we pulled out of the harbor the weather began to clear. If the weather did get too bad we could always stop in Bath and stay with Mrs. Myers till it blew over. Luckily for us, the *Black Duck* had enough speed to stay ahead of the storm.

We made it back to Blacks Harbour with no issues, but along the way I told Gus it was time to swap out the old Liberty with the one we bought from Kieran. I began to worry the old Liberty may fail us at an inconvenient time. Gus agreed and said he would help me swap the engines.

Mother was happy I was home again and I really needed the rest. The Fourth of July was coming up and everyone in Boston had the liquor they needed. I began to realize the holidays drove up consumption and I could see a cycle beginning to form. From there on I could almost plan when Joe would want liquor again and how much. I needed to be careful though because the Coast Guard probably knew the cycle also.

When we returned after the last load Mother told me that Father's poor memory condition would change frequently. Every once in a while Father's memory would return for a few days and he seemed to be normal again. Then, as abruptly as he gained his memory he would slip back into his forgetfulness again. Father would sometimes have normal conversations with Mother about everything and other times he would sit and gaze into space as if he didn't know where he was.

I was fortunate that while home this trip Father was coherent. I asked Father if he would help Gus and me swap the old Liberty for the new one. Father agreed and said he had a few ideas we could use for the *Black Duck*. Father said he wanted to think about what to do to the *Black Duck* a little more and that he would discuss it with Gus and me when Gus came over the next day. I was curious to hear what Father had in mind but I was willing to wait. He seemed like his old self again but I knew it probably wouldn't last too long.

The following day Gus and Byron came by the house early. Byron heard Father was feeling better and decided to spend a little time with him to talk about the businesses. Byron wanted to get Father's thoughts on some changes he wanted to make at the distillery. Since Prohibition was still being enforced Byron thought maybe the distillery should begin to cut back on production even further than before.

I think Byron was starting to worry about Gus and me running the liquor to Boston. I think he felt our luck might run out and we may get caught. I could understand his worry. We ran the last three loads back to back and did it with the old Liberty. Byron was right, something needed to change but I wasn't going to stop running the liquor. I believed if we swapped out the engines that would be sufficient to relieve everyone's worries.

That morning Father and Byron spent a lot of time together. After walking around the distillery they sat on the porch of the house for a long time and talked. I was beginning to think Byron had told Father about the side business of running liquor. I wasn't too concerned though because if Byron did tell Father, once his condition changed he would forget the discussion and it wouldn't matter.

Father and Byron called for Gus and me to join them on the porch. Mother had left for the day so it was only the four of us together.

Father began the conversation by telling me and Gus to sit down and explain to him what we were doing with the boat I bought from Captain John. As I began to speak, Byron, worried I wouldn't tell the truth, interrupted and said Father was aware of the arrangement I had with Joe in Boston. Father had actually figured out what we were doing with the liquor we were getting from the distillery.

Father realized based on how much time I was away from home and the amount of liquor the distillery was producing there was no way our Canadian customers were buying that much from us. There was no sense in keeping it a secret anymore. Mother, Father, Byron and I knew, without the sales to Boston, we wouldn't have kept the business profitable this long. Father also learned there was no more debt with the bank and that I had started a little nest egg to help keep the house and businesses running if Father began to have more serious health issues.

For some reason Father didn't mind what I was doing and kind of hinted he was proud of me for taking the risk and looking after the family and the businesses the way I did. He also said if it weren't for me running the liquor, Max would have not been able to stay in school at Boston. I then realized how intuitive Father really was. Father asked if Max knew what I was doing and I told him no. I felt if Max did know he would return home and make me stop.

I was relieved that Father knew what I was doing. Although running the whiskey was illegal I felt bad for keeping it from Father. After our talk Father asked if I would take him down to the docks to see the *Black Duck*. I didn't know what he was up to at the time but I didn't see any harm in taking him.

Father, Byron, Gus and I got into the truck and drove down to the docks. When we arrived I told Father I wanted to take the old Liberty out of the boat and install the new one I purchased from Shamus and Kieran in Boston. Father looked at me and said there would be plenty of time to do the swap but he wanted to see how well the boat ran. Gus went down to the water, jumped into the dingy and rowed out to the *Black Duck* and started it up. As usual it fired right up and Gus let it idle as we waited on shore.

Once the Liberty warmed up Gus pulled up the anchor and maneuvered the boat to us on shore. We all climbed aboard and took it out to open waters. Father went below deck, down to the Liberty and listened to it run. He yelled up to me in the pilothouse to give it more fuel. I obliged and we quickly picked up speed. There was the feeling again. The *Black Duck* had enough power while empty but I still wanted more speed for carrying bigger loads.

Father approached me in the pilothouse and told me there was nothing wrong with the old Liberty. He couldn't understand why I wanted to swap it out for the new one. I explained how I wanted to take bigger loads to Boston and he told me he had a better idea. I thought Father was going to tell me to get another boat and put the new Liberty in it but I was surprised to learn he had other ideas.

Byron and Father walked to the back of the boat and spoke for a little while. When they returned to Gus and me in the pilothouse Father told me in order to carry heaver loads and not loose speed we would need to increase the horsepower. With the Liberty's twelve cylinders and turbo-supercharger it was already putting out almost four hundred and fifty horsepower. I thought, how much more horsepower would we need? Swapping the engines wouldn't take care of that problem. In order to do it right, Father said, we would need to put both Liberties in the *Black Duck*.

At first I couldn't understand his reasoning but quickly realized, with both Liberty engines in the boat and almost nine hundred horsepower we could carry the heavier loads and also dramatically increase our speed. I couldn't imagine the *Black Duck* any faster than it was, but if Father was right we would have the fastest boat on the Atlantic Ocean, possibly the fastest boat in the world, and no one would be able to catch us.

Chapter Sixteen

Since most of the men employed by Father had experience working with boats he sent a few down to the dock to help Gus and me with the installation of the new Liberty. At first I thought it would be an easy job but then I learned from Father's workers there was a lot of preparation that needed to be done before the installation.

Father's employees taught me, with the increased horsepower the *Black Duck*'s internal structure would need to be reinforced. The higher speeds and heavier loads would put a lot of stress and strain on the boats hull and framework.

The first thing we did was to take the *Black Duck* out of the water and dry-dock it. We then removed the old Liberty engine and surveyed the internal structure of the boat for any possible weaknesses. Father's men showed me what to look for and how to strengthen and repair any problems that were found. Once we had the basic boat repairs completed we made drawings of where we would install the two Liberties and how the larger whiskey loads would be placed.

After drawing several rough sketches of where the two Liberty engines would be placed and the fact we would be carrying more whiskey cases than earlier runs, it became apparent the boat would require much more fuel than previously carried. In order to make the twin engine setup work well, we would have to carry all the liquor on deck.

I didn't care about carrying the whiskey on deck where it could be easily spotted because I anticipated Prohibition would end soon and it wouldn't matter anyway. Besides, with the two Liberties powering the *Black Duck* no one would be able to catch us even if they did see the whiskey on deck.

Although Father's employees knew much about boat building, it was still difficult to complete the installations of the Liberties. We had to build frames to cradle both engines and drill holes in the transom to relocate propeller shafts. We also needed to set up a larger cooling system to accommodate both Liberty engines.

Once we engineered the engine mounting framework and installed the Liberties we ran pipelines for the new cooling system. With this work completed it was just a matter of running the throttle cables and fuel lines so we could begin testing the *Black Duck* in the ocean.

I arranged to have the *Black Duck* placed back in the water so we could start the Liberties to see how they would run together. Once we had the boat back in the water we checked it for leaks and found the boat hardly drew in any water. The structural reinforcements must have tightened up the boat more than it was before.

We still had a lot of work to do before we were ready to transport any whiskey back to Boston. The fuel tank needed to be enlarged to carry more fuel or we would have to make several stops along the way to Boston to complete the trips. I didn't want to stop at all during the trips because that would increase our chances of being spotted by the Coast Guard. We never knew where the Coast Guard would be so I wanted to stay far from shore until I needed to come in to make the drop-off of liquor. I didn't want to take any more risks than needed.

The fuel tank was big enough to carry the additional fuel but it had to be modified since earlier, when I designed the fuel tank I set it up with a secret compartment to carry the whiskey. Now the secret compartment's extra space would be used for the additional fuel.

We had some fuel left over from the last trip back so I decided to start the Liberties to see how they would run. The old Liberty started easily but the new one gave us some trouble. The newer Liberty would crank over and start up but wouldn't continue to run. I took a few minutes to think back at what Albert taught me to see if I could figure out what the problem was.

I needed to think about the basics. What was needed to keep the engine running? Fuel and air, compression and spark, these were the basics. I knew I was getting fuel because I had already tested the fuel lines before starting the engines and the fuel pumps were working correctly. The turbo-supercharger was engaged so there was plenty of air being forced down the intake manifold. I didn't think compression was an issue because the engine was new and never run, so the only thing left was spark.

I removed the spark plugs and found they were all coated with oil. Apparently, in order to protect the Liberty's cylinder walls from rusting while in storage, the manufacturer put about a teaspoon of oil into each cylinder. I cleaned each spark plug and set the gap to the correct distance. Once this was completed the new Liberty started right up and ran as smoothly as the old Liberty.

Now we were back in business. Both Liberties were running perfectly as designed and the boat's structural changes were completed. All I needed to do was finish the fuel tank modification and we would be ready to take the *Black Duck* out to open waters and test it. I couldn't wait to see how fast the *Black Duck* would run in the ocean with the additional horsepower from the second Liberty.

After completing the fuel tank changes Gus and I left the docks and drove back to the house to get Father and Byron. We wanted them to come with us when we took the *Black Duck* out of the harbor. After all, it was Father and Byron who gave us the idea to put both Liberty engines in the boat. I would never have thought to put two engines in the boat. I would have settled for swapping out the old Liberty with the new and gone back to running the whiskey like before.

It was getting late in the day and Father asked if we could take the boat out the next morning. I was too excited about completing the work and wanted to see what the boat would do that day. Father convinced me we should wait so if we had trouble out on the water at least we wouldn't get stranded overnight. Although I still wanted to go out that late afternoon I took his advice and decided to wait.

The next morning I woke up early and jumped in the truck so I could pick up Gus and Byron at their house. I found Gus waiting for me in his front yard eager to go like me, but Byron was still eating his breakfast. Gus and I sat in the truck and talked about all the adventures and fun we were going to have with the new, faster *Black Duck*.

Byron finished eating, grabbed some tools from his shed and walked up to the truck. Byron asked why Father wasn't coming with us. I told him Father had a few things to do around the house before we left and would be ready when we returned to pick him up. When we got back to the house Father was waiting like promised and he also had a toolkit with him.

I asked Byron and Father why they brought tools with them. Didn't they have faith in us to get everything running right on the boat? They both said they had seen too many boats leave the docks and not come back. They said we would take a short ride around the harbor and if everything seemed to be running well then we could go out further to open the boat up and see how fast she would go.

When we arrived at the dock Captain John was waiting for us. He heard from some of the other boaters that the *Black Duck* was back in the water and that we would probably take it out for a test run. Captain John asked if he could come along and have his crew follow us in his new boat, just in case we needed a tow back. I didn't care who came along, I just wanted to get out on the water and play with the *Black Duck*.

I started up both Liberties and pulled up the anchor. Gus went below to check for leaks and came back up to report the boat was dry as a bone. Father asked me to take it slow for a little while so he and Captain John could go below to observe the Liberties. They were all beginning to drive me crazy. Not only did I have Father and Byron holding me back but now Captain John was on board and I was sure he would add his thoughts also.

We reached the fist buoy and as far as I could tell everything was running fine. Father yelled something up to me from below but I couldn't make out what he was saying. The exhaust of the two Liberties was much louder than I had anticipated. We would need to muffle the exhaust somehow before we could run whiskey back to Boston or we would give away our position if we came close to other boats or the Coast Guard.

Captain John sent Gus back up to the pilothouse to tell me to give the boat more throttle. Once I increased the throttle the noise from the exhaust grew louder and I couldn't believe how well the two engines responded. Both engines still seemed to be running fine. I circled the harbor a few times and sent Gus back below to ask Father if I could head out to open waters.

Gus, Father and Captain John all came back up on deck. Father and Captain John both agreed the Liberty engines were running very well together and that we shouldn't encounter any problems. Father, looking at me through the open pilothouse door, gave me a thumbs up and told me to increase our speed and head out to sea. Now we were going to have some fun like I wanted to.

We passed the last buoy in the harbor and had nothing in front of us but deep-blue sea. I continued to increase our speed a little at a time so Father wouldn't think I was too anxious. We were only at half throttle and already moving faster than full throttle when the *Black Duck* only had one engine. What a thrill it was to feel the speed and power of the two Liberty engines.

I couldn't believe how fast we were going. The bow of the *Black Duck* began to rise as I continued to move the throttle forward. It seemed as though there was no limit to how fast we could go. My legs began to shake from the excitement of going so fast. I had never experienced that feeling before that day and would never forget the look on Father's face.

I began to worry if I hit a wave incorrectly it might capsize the boat so I reduced the speed. Captain John approached me and told me not to worry and to go faster. He said the old boat was sturdy and could handle the speed. Captain John also told me that when we had a load of whiskey or anything else on deck it would steady the boat. With Captain John's boat slowly disappearing behind us I realized we had achieved the speed we were looking for.

I had seen enough, and besides, we didn't need to prove anything else that day. We accomplished what we wanted to do with the *Black Duck*. I believed the *Black Duck* was ready for the heavier loads I wanted to take to Boston and now it was just a matter of testing the boat with a full load of whiskey on board. I slowly turned the *Black Duck* around and headed back to the dock.

Captain John approached me and said I had done a good job fixing up his old boat. He told me if I ever wanted a real job he would definitely hire me to work with him and his crew. I reduced the throttle and asked Father to take over the controls so I could stand on deck. I walked to the back of the boat and stood there with Gus for a little while. We were both still amazed how fast the *Black Duck* now was. My legs were still shaking from the thrill of going so fast and I couldn't wait to do it again.

Chapter Seventeen

With the work completed on the *Black Duck* I could now get back to business. I paid my parents for the three loads of liquor I delivered to Boston to cover the cost of the building for the shelter. I also paid Father's workers and Gus for helping with the installation of the Liberties. I was nearly out of cash and needed to get back to work. I owned the building in Boston and I owned the *Black Duck* but that was it.

My parents' businesses were financially secure and if I could get Joe, Kieran and Shamus to buy more whiskey I could start saving money for Shannon and me. I contacted Shannon by telephone and asked her to let Shamus and Kieran know I was ready to return to Boston. I also let her know the *Black Duck* was now able to carry more cargo, possibly twice as much as earlier and asked Shannon to see if Joe was interested in hiring me again.

Shannon called me back a week later and asked me to come back to Boston with whatever cargo I could carry. She also told me to meet

Shamus and Kieran at the usual place and to be there in four days. Shamus told her to tell me to be on time, no later, no earlier.

During the nineteen twenties the economy in both Canada and the United States was booming. Stock prices were continually increasing and in some cases by over three times their actual value. Everyone wanted to be in on the stock market craze and banks were not reluctant to loan out money. In Canada there was no central banking system or monetary policy so banks could do what they wanted with their depositors' money. There was basically no intervention by the Canadian Government. Interest rates were high and people were borrowing money to buy stocks.

There was plenty of discretionary cash and people were spending it. Having the money to buy liquor wasn't a problem, getting the liquor was. In the short term I planned to make the most money I could bringing the liquor to Boston by boat. My only expense was buying the liquor from my parents and fueling the boat. Whatever was left I would give some to Gus and save the rest for me and Shannon. My goal was to run the shelter with Shannon and be happy for the rest of our lives.

Byron began to oversee the liquor operation at home and took care of whatever we needed. Byron had Father's men deliver the load of liquor to the docks so Gus and I didn't have to pick it up. I asked Byron to step up production at the distillery because I planned to make several trips to Boston. If I could cut my delivery time with the faster *Black Duck* I could have some free time and help Shannon run the shelter.

Gus and I made the first shipment of the larger load to Boston in just over twelve hours. We couldn't believe how fast the *Black Duck* was even under the weight of the heavier load. Each of the last three smaller loads took us over twenty hours to deliver. During this trip I calculated we had the *Black Duck* easily traveling at almost forty knots. I couldn't wait to see how quick we could get back to Blacks Harbour with no cargo on board.

We met up with Kieran and Shamus exactly the day they were expecting us. This time Shamus brought several trucks and more men to help offload the liquor. It was much easier to empty the *Black Duck* without having to pull the liquor out of the cargo hole. Storing the liquor on deck allowed us to get into shore, offload, and back out to sea in no time. Even Kieran was impressed.

Kieran paid me sixty-five thousand dollars for the larger load of liquor. I actually thought he was being generous. I would have taken less money, because to me this was easy money. Kieran then asked me how soon we could bring more. I told him based on the amount of liquor the distillery could produce I could easily make two trips a month. Kieran said he would pay the same, sixty-five thousand dollars for each bigger load, twice a month. I didn't expect him to agree so quickly. He must have had more customers and needed it badly, or his other liquor sources were not delivering.

After collecting the money, Gus and I set out for Rockport to refuel and to call Shannon. When I contacted Shannon she was happy to hear from me. I asked her to send the boy from Albert's filling station to Rockport, with the truck, to pick us up. I planned to leave the *Black Duck* behind, hidden so no one would find it. Leaving the boat hidden after each delivery would become our normal routine from now on. Shannon would know what day and time I would meet Shamus and Kieran and she would make arrangements for the boy to drive to Rockport after we offloaded the liquor.

When the boy arrived with the truck we set out for Boston. Gus and I drove the boy back to Albert's filling station and went to the shelter to see how things were going. I was happy to see Shannon again and pleased to see the shelter was running well. There was plenty of volunteer staff to look after the boys so Shannon spent most of her time managing the donated supplies and the upkeep on the building.

Shannon loved helping the boys. I saw a different woman in Shannon when I returned that trip. She was so patient with her staff and the boys. She was a hard worker and earned much respect from everyone. I liked the woman I was seeing very much. It gave me great pride to know someday she would be at my side always. Shannon had such a warm glow around her that afternoon. She looked so beautiful.

Shannon and I spent the remainder of the afternoon together. She brought me up to speed on everything that was going on at the shelter. Shannon remarked on how helpful everyone was who volunteered and how the local merchants donated so much. The homeless boys seemed to be very grateful for what Shannon had done for them. Some of the older boy who found jobs decided to move into an apartment on their own but continued to return to the shelter to help with the younger children.

Shannon also told me that her sister was working at the restaurant full time now. Since Mary now took over Shannon's job at the restaurant, Shannon didn't need to work there anymore. Shannon dedicated almost all of her time at the shelter and to being with Mary. Shannon enjoyed having Mary around. Shannon was lonely for the rest of her family but never said anything to me. Shannon and Mary spoke about having their parents return to Boston from New York so they could all be together.

While with Shannon that afternoon I gave her ten thousand dollars from the money Kieran paid me that morning. I told her to keep it for the shelter and herself in case an emergency came up. I also told Shannon I would be bringing two loads of liquor each month for Kieran and Shamus and that I would continue to provide money for her to put away, or to use for whatever she needed it for. I still had plenty for myself and wanted to make sure she wouldn't have to worry about money.

Now that I was leaving the *Black Duck* near Rockport and driving into Boston, Gus and I needed a place to stay. I asked Shannon to find an apartment for me and Gus close to the shelter. With Mary, Carol and Shannon all living at the apartment upstairs from the restaurant it was most likely crowded. I suspected Shannon was spending late hours at the shelter but she didn't want to say anything to me about it. While I was away Shannon could stay at my apartment to make life easier for herself. It would also give Carol and Mary more room for themselves at the apartment in the restaurant.

Everything fell into place perfectly but life started to move really fast. I had a lot of things going on. I couldn't become complacent. I still had the Coast Guard to worry about and they weren't going away anytime soon. In fact, the Coast Guard started stepping up more patrols. As long as I left the *Black Duck* near Rockport I hoped no one suspected me of bringing the liquor to Boston.

Between the summers of nineteen twenty-seven and nineteen twenty-eight I brought twenty-four loads of liquor to Kieran and Shamus. I made more money than I could have ever imagined. I began to worry what to do with all the cash. I gave most of it to Mr. Jacobs to hold for me at the bank in Blacks Harbour. Mr. Jacobs told me I should buy property instead of holding cash.

I spoke to Albert to see if he thought it was a good idea to buy property. Albert explained to me how the rent collected from tenants would cover my costs and should leave a little left over. Since Albert was on the deed with Shannon for the shelter in Boston I asked him if he would help me buy some more buildings and have the deeds in their names. He seemed a little hesitant at first but decided he would help me. It was nice to know I had Albert to help me out.

Albert found three buildings in Boston which already had tenants. I decided to buy all three and let him manage them. I made a deal with him to keep some money collected from the rents and to give any extra left over to Shannon for expenses she might have at shelter. I also had Mr. Jacobs use some of the money I left in the bank to buy farmland back in Blacks Harbour. I had Byron use the parcels to grow more wheat and crops for the distillery.

I couldn't have planned things better than how they turned out. Things were going so well that I actually started contemplating not running liquor anymore. By this point I realized I wasn't running liquor for the money, I was doing it for the adventure. It had more to do with living your dreams, doing what you loved to do and getting as much out of life as you possibly could.

Being with Gus on the water and traveling back and forth between home and Boston was very peaceful and calming in this new, fast-paced life. Fortunately, we hadn't had any encounters with the Coast Guard and as long as I was careful I had nothing to worry about. I'm sure the Coast Guard was looking for me by now but with the speed of the *Black Duck* they would have to be lucky if they wanted to catch me. I knew no one could catch the *Black Duck* in open waters. We were just too fast.

The speed of the *Black Duck* and the adventure of eluding the Coast Guard was such a great thrill. It was almost addictive. Knowing I could go anywhere I wanted and do whatever I wanted enhanced the thrill. The responsibility I felt when I started running liquor to help my parents and to make sure there was enough money for Max to continue school was all but gone. Even the shelter was running well and didn't need any involvement from me.

Chapter Eighteen

Another year had come and gone. It was now early spring, nineteen twenty-nine, and I had just completed another twenty-four or twenty-five more runs of liquor to Boston. I sold a lot of liquor but the mood in the States started to change. I was only twenty-one years old and wealthy. The word on the street was the Government was really going to start cracking down heavily on illegal booze, precipitated by a deadly shootout between rival gangs in Chicago.

Al Capone planned to wipe out Bugs Moran and most of the North Side Gang to eliminate his competition. To lure Bugs Moran in he made it appear a low-price load of whiskey was in a warehouse in Chicago. The price was too irresistible for Moran to turn down. With most of the North Side Gang already inside the warehouse Moran showed up late and saw a Chicago police wagon pull up outside the warehouse. Moran and his bodyguards, thinking it was a raid for the liquor, drove off, leaving his men behind.

It turned out the men who Moran thought were police were only in disguise. Three hit men disguised as police and several other plainclothes men executed Moran's gang. Many suspected Capone's henchmen did the killing but Moran got away. Because it happened on February fourteenth, the hit was known as the St. Valentine's Massacre.

The gangs had their own law on the street and the Federal Government needed to put a stop to it. The great wealth these gangs acquired from liquor and other organized crimes was worth protecting. The gangs controlled entire cities and weren't going to give it up easily. The Federal Government was going to have to take back control if they wanted to stop the gangs. The Federal Government assembled all available men to rid the country of illegal liquor distribution and sales, and organized crime. The Federal agents were called G-men, short for Government men. No one could be trusted anymore after that day. The United States became divided. Its citizens were split between crime and the law.

It became evident more blood was going to be shed between rival gangs to get control over the liquor so I decided to stop the transportation of it. It just became too risky to move anything. Now, I had gangs, G-men and the Coast Guard to worry about. Shamus and Kieran became very angry with me for telling them I wouldn't be bring any more liquor from Canada but I had the liquor and I had the way to bring it, I was now calling the shots. I didn't want to do it anymore.

When Joe found out from Kieran and Shamus I wasn't bringing any more liquor he told them to get me and bring me to the restaurant. A few days later Joe and I met in the afternoon and I planned on letting him know I wanted out. I owed no one anything and I couldn't be forced to bring more liquor. When I arrived at the restaurant Joe motioned for me to follow him to the back room. Once again we went down the hatch and into the bar below. He sat me down at a table and poured two shots of whiskey. Joe pushed one towards me and lifted the other glass as though to salute.

As I picked up my shot Joe moved his hand forward and tipped my glass. He drank his shot and I did the same immediately after. With a big smile on his face Joe told me my father made the best whiskey he ever tasted. He also said, "It sure was a nice ride, wasn't it, kid?" Joe knew it was over, and we both made a lot of money. We didn't need to be greedy. G-men were watching everyone and we were no exception. It was time to stop running liquor before we lost everything.

Although Joe had a smile on his face there was still something bothering him. He asked me if I invested any money in the stock market and, if I had, I needed to sell it, everything! Joe said, "Convert all your stock to cash and whatever money you have in a bank, get it out." I asked Joe why I needed to do it but he wouldn't tell me anything else. Joe said, "Someday you're going to owe me a favor for this information." I had no idea what the hell he was talking about. Owe him a favor, for what?

My gut feeling was telling me Joe knew something was going to happen in the stock market and for some reason he was looking after me. After the meeting with Joe I went to see Shannon and told her what he said. Shannon said she had invested money Albert was sending her and that she would sell all her stock. I called Mr. Jacobs in Canada to let him know I planned to buy more buildings in Boston and that I would be returning to Blacks Harbour soon to get some of my money. I only told Mr. Jacob I was buying more property so he wouldn't become suspicious as to why I was pulling my money out of the bank.

Shannon cashed out the stocks she owned and I returned home to take my money out of the bank. I had over a million dollars sitting in the bank entrusted to Mr. Jacobs. I brought the crate I took the new Liberty engine out of and drove to town to see Mr. Jacobs. I pulled around the back of the bank so Gus and I could load the cash into the crate. We took the crate and money back to the farm and locked it in the shed. There the money would be safe, and only Gus and I would know where it was and only we would have access to it.

It was now March, nineteen twenty-nine, and Herbert Hoover had just been inaugurated as the President of the United States. Problems with the stock market began to surface around March twenty-fifth, with small crashes and recoveries on Wall Street. Hoover and economists were having closed door discussions about the stock market and the economy but they didn't intervene to prevent any problems. Many investors began to panic and started a selling frenzy. Fortunately for me and Shannon, Joe's advice paid off, all our money was safe.

During that summer the economic situation seemed to stabilize, but as autumn approached the United States economy took a serious downturn. Then the unthinkable happened. On October twenty-fourth panic selling of stocks started a crash on Wall Street and by October twenty-ninth the stock market collapsed. Financial centers in the United States and Canada were ruined. Fortunes were lost almost overnight. People were actually jumping out of buildings to commit suicide because of their debts.

I went back to Boston to be with Shannon and to see how the shelter was managing. With so much poverty, homeless children started coming out of the woodwork. Families couldn't care for their young children and sent them to Shannon to stay at the shelter. There just wasn't enough room at the shelter for everyone.

Because of the situation with the stock market, two tenants from my buildings in Boston went out of business. Since the buildings were now empty, Shannon asked if she could use them temporarily as shelters until she could figure out what to do with all the boys. Although she said she only needed the buildings temporarily I had a feeling it might be awhile. Since I wouldn't be able to find new tenants soon I didn't have any issues with Shannon using the buildings.

Now there were three shelters to run. I had no idea how Shannon was going to manage all the work but knew she would somehow find a way. It was going to become difficult, especially with winter approaching. Christmas was only a few weeks away and as the cold weather set in the homeless situation became worse. Local merchants weren't donating supplies anymore and there were just too many mouths to feed.

Kieran, while helping with the shelters, could see we were running low on supplies. Kieran said he could get some cots, clothes and food for the children but it wouldn't be free. Shannon had depleted her money and all of my cash was sitting in the shed at home. I thought if I could borrow some money I would save a trip home but didn't know who to ask. Kieran said he would arrange for the supplies to be dropped off at Albert's filling station that night but he would only give me twenty-four hours to come up with the money. Kieran said if I didn't have the money the next day he would sell the supplies to others who wanted it.

The next morning when I arrived at Albert's filling station I found the supplies Shannon needed. I asked Albert if he could loan me some money but he said he couldn't. Albert said the only one he knew who had the amount of cash I needed was Joe. I didn't want to rely on Joe anymore but it looked like I had no choice. I called Joe's secretary, Elizabeth, and she said she would relay the message. I waited for a few hours for Joe or Elizabeth to call back but didn't hear back from either of them.

I was just about to go to my apartment when Joe pulled up to the filling station. Albert left Joe and me alone in the office while he helped some customers. Joe told me Elizabeth said I wanted to borrow some money and that even he couldn't get his hands on any cash. I argued with Joe and told him he owed me for all I had done for him. Joe lashed out at me and said if it wasn't for him I wouldn't have any money. I had never seen Joe so angry before.

Joe quickly stood up and reminded me about the time a few months earlier when he told me to take all my money out of the stock market and the bank. He was right, most banks had no money to give depositors after the stock market crash and quite a few banks closed their doors for good. I wouldn't have been able to get my money out of the bank back in Canada unless I did it before the crash. Now I knew what Joe meant when he told me earlier I would thank him later for the advice he gave me and that I would owe him for it.

Joe said, the way he saw it I had three choices. I could go home and get my money but I probably wouldn't make it back in time to pay Kieran, I could forget about the supplies and let the children keep sleeping on the floor and go cold and hungry, or he would take care of the debt with Kieran but I would have to agree to do Joe a few favors. I thought Joe wanted me to go home to get a more loads of liquor but he said what he had in mind would be much easier.

Joe said a ship from England was expected to arrive off the coast in a few days carrying liquor for him. The British ship, *Symor*, would be anchored fifteen miles off Cape Cod and all I had to do was go get the liquor and bring it back to the beach house near Rockport. Joe said Shamus and Kieran would wait for me like usual and they would take the liquor from there. I told Joe that Gus and I would need help loading the liquor from the *Symor* so he said he would arrange for some men to meet us in Rockport to come with us to help.

I didn't think it would be a problem to run out to the *Symor*, then run back in. With a few helpers we should be able to pick up and drop off the liquor in a few hours. Gus and I went back to Rockport to get the *Black Duck* so we could meet the *Symor*. There were three men waiting for us just like Joe promised. The five of us went out to the *Symor* and loaded the *Black Duck* with the liquor. When we arrived at the beach house Shamus and Kieran were waiting just as expected. The three men who came with Gus and I offloaded the liquor, then stayed with Shamus and Kieran when we left. It was easier than I thought.

With the supplies from Kieran Shannon was able to arrange a nice Christmas for the boys at the shelters. The boys were happy to get warm clothes, food and cots to sleep on. Shannon wondered how I was able to get supplies so quickly since she had tried and no one would donate anything. I told her about the trip out to the *Symor* and she wanted to know why I didn't tell here sooner. I told Shannon I didn't want her to worry and that it wasn't that difficult.

Shannon made me promise her I would always tell her where I was and what I was doing. I didn't think it was a big deal so I promised her I would always let her know. Although it didn't take me very long to get the liquor from the *Symor* I needed to be careful. With the New Year approaching there was a good chance the waters surrounding Boston were being watched by the Coast Guard.

Chapter Nineteen

A week before the New Year Joe stopped by the shelter to see how Shannon and I were managing. Joe approached me while I was alone and said the *Symor* was coming back from Bermuda with another load of liquor for him to buy and he needed someone to go get it. He asked if I was interested in picking up the liquor and said if I did this load, he would see to it the shelters had everything they needed until winter passed.

I couldn't imagine why Joe was being so generous. I know Boston was dry, but with the New Year only a week away I guessed Joe had a chance to make a lot of money with this load. I told Joe I thought it was too risky to bring any liquor into Boston. Joe said I was right. He knew the beach house was being watched and that he wanted me to bring the liquor to Newport, Rhode Island. He told me he would have an empty boat go to the beach house in Rockport, the same night I would meet the *Symor*, to throw the Coast Guard off my trail.

The *Symor* was scheduled to return on December twenty-eighth and all I had to do was pull up alongside her, load the liquor and head south. Joe said he would have the three helpers meet me in Rockport again so we could load the liquor quickly and get out. The plan was to bring the load to Newport, where another boat would meet us to take the liquor.

The ocean was calm that December night, with some patchy fog, and visibility was poor. It was better for us with the fog. I didn't like to be on the water at night in an unfamiliar area but if we ran without lights no one would see us at all. I wanted to stay away from the dock in Rockport with the *Black Duck* so around seven o'clock that night Gus and I, with the truck, picked up the three men Joe said would be waiting for us.

We then drove to the place where I hid the *Black Duck* and shoved off around eight that evening. We headed south in the *Black Duck* to meet the *Symor* off Cape Cod. We waited at the spot where we met the *Symor* during the first trip, but it wasn't there. I thought I had made a mistake and read the charts wrong so I rechecked. We were in the right place on the right day but the *Symor* wasn't there. I waited till ten but there was still no sign of the *Symor*. It started to get very windy and cold in the open ocean, so the five of us huddled in the pilothouse to keep warm.

Around eleven o'clock I decided there was no reason to wait any longer—the *Symor* wasn't showing up and it was too cold to just sit out there. I started up the Liberties and turned the *Black Duck* north to get back to shore. About thirty minutes later we came across the *Symor*. It had been waiting in the wrong place with her lights off.

I started feeling uncomfortable as we approached the big ship. Was she stopped by the Coast Guard? Was the Coast Guard waiting for us on board? There was no activity on deck and her lights were out. We weren't carrying anything illegal so there was nothing anyone could do to us. When we pulled up alongside the *Symor* someone dropped a rope down to us. Once the captain of the *Symor* recognized the *Black Duck* he turned the deck lights on.

It was around one o'clock in the morning by the time we had

transferred the load to the *Black Duck*. We had taken on about four hundred sacks of assorted liquor. I wondered if it was too late to meet up with the other boat waiting for us in Newport. Once again, we headed south and I kept my fingers crossed the other boat would be waiting. I wasn't familiar with the waters around Narragansett Bay, so as we drew closer I turned off our lights and headed in slowly.

I needed to find a landmark but the fog had thickened. It became difficult to see. I was relying on our charts to keep us offshore but had no reference point. The charts showed a buoy near the southwest part of the inlet. I stopped the *Black Duck* for a moment and shut down the Liberties. We could hear a faint ring in the distance just north of us. It had to be the Dumpling Rock Bell buoy. If we could locate the buoy we were home free.

I could see the men were getting tired so I sped up the *Black Duck*. We all huddled in the pilothouse as we slowly approached the sound of the bell. About two hundred yards from the buoy, I could make out the partial outline of a bigger boat through the fog. It was around two o'clock in the morning, who else would be out here this late? It must have been the boat Joe said would meet us. The boat had its lights out and was tied to the buoy.

About twenty-five yards from the ship, the captain of the other boat turned on her lights and pointed a large searchlight on us. I had seen that light before. I now recognized the shape of the ship. It was the Coast Guard vessel CG-290. Since the Coast Guard was tied to the buoy there was no way they could get us. I sped up the *Black Duck* and headed straight for the cutter. I passed its bow at full speed and swerved off, emitting a black smoke screen to conceal us. The cutter rocked violently from the wake I had created when I turned sharply.

The captain of the cutter, sounding his horn to signal us to stop, was powerless. I sped away at full speed and swerved the *Black Duck* to the right then back to the left. We couldn't see the Coast Guard anymore but all of a sudden I heard the rattle of machine-gun fire. The sound was horrifying and lasted only a few seconds. The bullets fired riddled through the pilothouse as pieces of wood chips flew everywhere. Of the three men who were on board to help us, two men fell instantly to the deck and one slumped back against the wall. As the wounded man who fell backwards slid down to the deck I saw streaks of his blood left on the wall. This wasn't supposed to happen.

The Coast Guard, by now untied from the buoy, would quickly come after us. My body shook as I steered the *Black Duck* towards shore to get away. For some reason I hadn't been hit by any of the bullets. As we drew closer to shore I shut down the engines and checked on the men who had fallen to the floor. My mind was racing. What the hell happened? Two men were dead and the third would soon be if he didn't get help soon.

Now I realized what it really felt like to be scared. I looked at Gus in fear and said, "What did I do? I didn't mean for anyone to die." Gus told me to get off the *Black Duck* and he would take the three men back to the Coast Guard for help. Gus said he had been hit in the hand and also needed help. As I jumped to shore I had no idea where I was going. Gus started the *Black Duck* and backed away from shore. As he looked back at me he saluted as if to say he'd be okay. I could see blood streaming down his arm as he and the *Black Duck* disappeared into the dark night.

How could everything have gone so wrong so quickly? I needed to get to town so I could find a way back to Boston. I wondered how Gus would make out with the Coast Guard. I could see the spotlight from the Coast Guard slowly approaching. I watched through the fog as the *Black Duck* drifted up and bumped against the cutter.

I could hear the commotion of the Guardsmen shouting down to Gus as several of the Coast Guardsmen boarded the *Black Duck*. There was nothing more I could do for him now. I only hoped that he could get the medical help he needed and wouldn't go to prison. He was on his own and so was I. The sun started coming up and I didn't want to be seen by the Coast Guards so I started running. I didn't know where I was going or what I was going to do but I had to find my way back to Boston.

As I approached Jamestown I hailed down a truck and asked him where he was going. He looked at me and could see something was terribly wrong. The truck driver asked me what had happened and why I was wet. I told him I had problems with my boat offshore and needed a ride home to get help. The driver said he could take me as far as Providence but after that I would need to find another ride. While we waited for the ferry to arrive to take us to Newport the driver pulled a blanket out from behind the seat to keep me warm.

After reaching Newport we drove north to Providence. While we drove along the road I closed my eyes, hoping it was all just a bad dream. Over and over again I kept hearing the sounds of the machine-gun fire and envisioned the men falling to the deck. I still couldn't believe what had just happened. I wanted the sounds and thoughts to go away but they wouldn't. What would I tell Gus's mother and Byron? How would I explain to Joe I lost his load? And Shannon, I know she didn't want me to run any more liquor, how would I explain this to her?

When we arrived in Providence I found a telephone to call Kieran. I remembered Kieran telling me if I ever needed help I could call him. As I held the phone I couldn't stop my body from shaking. I was still scared and didn't know what to say. When Kieran answered the telephone the words wouldn't come out of my mouth. Kieran kept saying, "Who is this?" and I finally replied, "It's me." Kieran could tell something was wrong. He told me to tell him where I was and not to go anywhere. He would come and get me.

About two hours later Kieran and Shamus showed up. I didn't know how to explain to them that I lost the *Black Duck* and the load of liquor. They told me they already knew what happened to me and Gus. The Coast Guard had been hunting the *Black Duck* for over a year, and now that it was caught word spread fast of the capture. I asked them if they knew anything about the three men and Gus. Kieran said all three men died and Gus was in a hospital in Fort Adams.

Shamus wanted to know if Gus would say anything about him, Kieran and Joe. I said I didn't think Gus would give us away. They both looked at me in disgust and said he had better not for my sake. I asked Kieran if he would take me to see Shannon. Shamus said he would let her know I was okay but that I couldn't stay in town. They said if Gus said anything, the first place the Coast Guard would look for me is in Boston. The rest of the ride to Boston was quiet.

When we arrived in Boston Kieran dropped Shamus off at the restaurant and took me to Albert's filling station. We were only there long enough for me to change into some dry clothes. While Kieran waited for me in the automobile I explained to Albert what had happened. I asked him to let Shannon know I was going to be all right and I would call her as soon as I could. Albert opened the cash register and gave me a fistful of money. At the time I didn't know how much it was or how far it would take me but I told him I would pay him back for all his help.

Kieran drove me to the train station and told me to lay low for a while. He told me not to go home in case Gus told the Coast Guard who I was. When I boarded the train the only place I could think of to go was Mrs. Myers's house in Bath. No one knew me in Bath and I was sure no one would look for me there. Kieran told me to call him in a few days and he would tell me if he had any other news. I told Kieran I was scared and he just looked at me. He said to snap out of it. There was nothing I could do for Gus and that I had to take care of myself now.

The train ride to Bath seemed to take forever. It snowed heavily the entire time and it wasn't letting up. The ride to Bath was slow and it gave me lots of time to think about what I was going to do. I had to let my parents know where I was so they wouldn't worry. I also needed to let them know about Gus. I was still scared. I had acted like a man when I was making lots of money but in reality I was still a twenty-one-year-old kid. How was I going to get myself out of this mess?

It was dark when I reached Bath and the snow was piled high on the road. The streets were nearly impassable as I walked to Mrs. Myers's house. As I walked slowly through the high snow a calm feeling came over me. Something inside was telling me Gus was going to be all right. I hoped the feeling was right. When I reached Mrs. Myers's house the lights were still on so I rang the bell on the front door. I could see a fire dwindling in the fire place through a window on the front porch. Mrs. Myers answered the door and was surprised to see me.

Mrs. Myers invited me in and asked me to throw a few logs on the fire. She could see I was shaking and thought it was from the cold so she went to the kitchen to get me something warm to drink. As I sat by the warmth of the fireplace Mrs. Myers returned with some coffee. I was exhausted for all that had happened that day. My body began to slowly stop shaking and soon after, I had fallen asleep. When I awoke the next morning I was still on Mrs. Myers's couch.

I thought I had dreamt everything about being caught by the Coast Guard but when I called out for Gus he didn't answer. Mrs. Myers came down the stairs and told me I came alone the night before and Gus wasn't with me. Now I knew what happened was real.

Chapter Twenty

As the nineteen twenties ended in financial disaster I thought I was immune from its backlash since I had taken my money out of the bank like Joe suggested. I never thought I would get caught by the Coast Guard and lose the *Black Duck*. The worst part was, three men lost their lives and the fate of my best friend Gus was unknown, all because of me. I never should have agreed to make that last liquor run.

I was stuck in Bath, Maine, and had no way to get out. All the roads were still impassable because of the heavy snowfall. I walked into town so I could find a telephone to call Kieran. I wanted to see if there was any news about Gus. When I finally got a hold of Kieran by telephone he told me to buy a local newspaper. Apparently the capture of the *Black Duck* made the headlines all over the country. The US Government wanted to show they were coming after everyone dealing in illegal liquor and were not going to let up.

The newspaper story told how it was by sheer luck that the Coast Guard encountered the *Black Duck* and its illegal cargo of liquor. On the afternoon of December twenty-eighth, two Coast Guard cutters, the CG-290 and CG-241, left the New London, Connecticut Coast Guard base to set up patrol along the eastern passage of Rhode Island's Narragansett Bay. The Coast Guard vessels were specifically sent to look for and prevent any rum runners from entering the area.

Boatswain Alexander C. Cornell skippered the CG-290 and his crew consisted of several men. Cornell was an experienced officer who resigned his commission in the US Navy to join the Coast Guard. Cornell had over sixteen years combined service in the Navy and Coast Guard and knew the New England waters very well. Boatswain Cornell and his men were known for capturing many boats carrying illegal liquor. Their most famous seizure, up until the *Black Duck*, was the *Idle Hour*, which was converted into CG-918.

CG-241, the Coast Guard cutter that escorted Cornell's boat, was anchored off the Narragansett channel near Fort Adams and Cornell took his patrol boat to the area across the channel known as Dumpling Rock. That evening, because of the depth of the waters near Dumpling Rock, Cornell tied a line to the Dumpling Rock Bell Buoy and shut off all her lights. The news report continued to say the *Black Duck*, a sturdy-built wooden speedboat, had just taken a load from the British ship *Symor* and was heading into Narragansett Bay when Cornell and his crew heard the sound of the *Black Duck*'s powerful Liberty engines approaching. Cornell waited patiently until the *Black Duck* was nearly upon him. With his bright spotlight turned on and focused towards the *Black Duck*, Cornell signaled for the rum runner to stop.

Cornell was quoted as saying his men were in imminent danger because it appeared as though the *Black Duck*, with its lights doused and at full speed, was preparing to ram his vessel. Just before impact, the *Black Duck* swerved away and let out a smoke screen. The *Black Duck* had eluded the Coast Guard for over a year and Cornell was determined to stop her. Cornell ordered his gunner to fire warning shots over the *Black Duck*'s bow. Just as the gunner pulled the trigger and released a burst of twenty-one shots in about three seconds, the *Black Duck* steered into the oncoming bullets, which penetrated the port side of the boat and pilothouse.

I had a hard time reading the rest of the story, I knew what had happened. The report went on to say Captain Cornell didn't intentionally fire to hurt anyone. It was just a warning in accordance with Coast Guard regulations. But in the end, three men were dead and one had a serious injury to his hand. Gus, the injured man, was first cared for on the cutter GC-290 and then taken immediately to Fort Adams to be interrogated.

At Fort Adams Gus said he and the three men were hired hands who didn't know they were out to get liquor. Because of the state of the economy, Gus said he was only trying to make some money so he could eat. Cornell said one of his men saw the captain of the *Black Duck* jump overboard and go to shore. Since Gus wasn't the captain of the *Black Duck* and no one knew who the owner was, he was released without charges and sent back to Canada. Boatswain Cornell said his mission was only to capture the vessels and stop the illegal transportation of liquor.

After the *Black Duck* was seized and inspected the Coast Guard discovered why it was so elusive. Because of the unique size and weight of the wooden boat and strength of the *Black Duck*'s two Liberty engines, the Coast Guard realized there was no faster boat on the water. Cornell planned to convert the *Black Duck* to a cutter and knew with it he could outrun any other boat. I carried that newspaper article around with me for over five years and somehow lost it during my travels.

While in Bath I tried reaching Shannon several times by telephone but for some reason I couldn't get a hold of her. I thought she must have been busy with the shelters so I decided to call Albert. I was able to reach Albert and asked him if he let Shannon know I was all right. Albert said Shannon was aware that I was okay and that I shouldn't worry about her. He also said I shouldn't come back to Boston for a while.

Albert told me, after the *Black Duck* was captured and news headlines told of the three men who were killed, riots flared up in Boston and New London, Connecticut. Coast Guard recruiting posters were torn down in Boston and windows were shattered at the recruiting station after a protest meeting. Not only were the civilians mad about the three deaths, their supply of liquor had been shut down.

In New London the situation was worse. When the *Black Duck* was brought to port a gang brutally beat two Coast Guardsmen. During the first eight years of Prohibition no civilians were ever injured or killed over liquor. The only deaths reported during this time were of rival mobsters fighting for control over the distribution and sales of the illegal liquor. These scenes in Massachusetts and Connecticut inspired uprisings in other parts of the United States and caught the attention of the Federal Government.

It became clear to everyone, more US citizens had grown tired of Prohibition than were for it, especially since the Government was spending hundreds of millions of dollars to enforce it and people were starving due to the economic depression.

I couldn't understand why all this was happening. In Europe, countries had just fought to save themselves from being taken over by aggressor countries and in the US and Canada we brought hardship upon ourselves because of greed. We created our own problems between the Government and its civilians and somehow it had to end.

Several times I seriously thought about turning myself in so the fighting would end but I would have to implicate everyone involved. It would include Shannon, and if she were arrested, who would manage the shelters? Albert told me it was a ridiculous idea and as it was, Shannon was probably already being watched. He also said her friend Captain Scully had approached her about the *Black Duck* incident and wanted to know if she knew anything about it.

Now I understood why Shannon wasn't taking my telephone calls. She was trying to protect me from being caught. I knew Shannon had her hands full with running the shelters and didn't need me causing her any problems. I had to sit tight like Kieran told me and wait for everything to settle down.

Shannon's only income to help run the shelters was the money I provided and some donations. Somehow I had to get back to Blacks Harbour so I could make arrangements with Mr. Jacobs at the bank to send her money on a regular basis. Since Gus was deported back to Canada and he was the only one who knew where I hid my money I would need his help.

I called Mr. Jacobs and told him what had happened to me, Gus and the *Black Duck*. He told me he was aware of the seizure of the *Black Duck* and the injury to Gus. Gus had told everyone I was safe but didn't know where I was. He presumed I had fled back to Canada but when he arrived I wasn't there. I asked Mr. Jacobs if Father and Mother knew what happened and he said yes because the local papers carried the story.

Gus let everyone know I wasn't hurt but also said he did not know where I was. Since I could trust Mr. Jacobs I let him know I was in Bath and could not get home because of the heavy snowfall. Mr. Jacobs asked if there was anything he could do to help. I asked if he could loan me some money until I returned home and to set up a transfer to a Boston bank to help Shannon with the shelters. I told him I would have someone contact him to make the arrangements.

After the conversation with Mr. Jacobs I called Albert again to let him know I would need his help with the money transfer. I told him to go to Joe's bank and set up an account as if an anonymous donor was making a contribution. Albert agreed to help and said he would contact Mr. Jacobs directly to set up the transfer. I told Albert I would have Mr. Jacobs send five thousand dollars a month to the account and no repayment would be required. I had no use for the money and my dream was to help the homeless children.

Shannon didn't need to know it was me sending the money. Once the transfer was completed there would be no reason for me to get involved. I only hoped the five thousand dollars would be enough to help keep the shelters running until I could come up with another plan. I was sure Shannon would know how to make the money last.

Chapter Twenty-One

Not until March, during the winter of nineteen thirty, did the snow begin to melt. I had to get out of Bath soon and return home. I liked Mrs. Myers and living in the quiet town but it was starting to drive me crazy. There were still lots of things I needed to do and I had no resources in Maine. I worked off my room and board at Mrs. Myers's house by working at the ship yard and doing odd jobs around the town. Everyone seemed happy to have me around to help and no one asked me where I was from.

I purchased a ticket to Canada as soon as the ferry started running again. This trip home would be much different than any other time before. In a way I didn't want to go home. I felt like a failure for losing the *Black Duck* and for almost getting Gus and myself killed. I didn't know how I was going to explain it to everyone. In the back of my mind I always knew running the liquor could be dangerous but I never imagined it would turn out the way it did.

When I arrived home I walked into town. I had a large overcoat on with a scarf that covered my face. I didn't want anyone in town to see me because I knew they would ask questions. I only wanted to get home to see my father and mother and to see if Gus was all right. I didn't want to stop and call home for someone to come get me and since Gus lived closer to town I walked to his house. When I arrived no one was there except Byron. He asked me to come inside for a while to warm up while he dressed. He asked me how I was and if I needed anything. I told Byron I was fine and just wanted to go home.

Byron told me Gus and his mother were at my house that evening and he was planning to drive over in a short while. They were all invited over for dinner that night. Byron had just gotten out of work and went home first to clean up and change. I asked him how everyone was and he said everyone was worried about me. I asked about Gus and he said Gus was doing all right. His hand had healed and he was back working at the distillery again.

After Byron changed we drove to my house. It was dark now and as we approached the house I could see silhouettes of people standing in the parlor around the fireplace. I had hoped the house would be quiet when I returned but it didn't look that way. As we drove up the driveway I could see someone peering through the curtains at us. It looked like Gus but I wasn't sure.

Byron parked the truck around the side of the house and we walked in together. Just as we entered the house, everyone yelled, "Surprise!" It was Byron's birthday and the dinner was just an excuse to get him to the house that evening. I think the surprise was on everyone else when I walked in the door behind Byron. It was such a nice reunion. Mother was crying and Father shook my hand when I approached him. It was a bit strange coming home but the birthday party and everyone we loved around made me feel much better. I was still ashamed about what had happened to Gus but no one mentioned anything to me about it that evening.

Gus came up to me and gave me a big bear hug. He said there was another surprise and went to the kitchen. When he returned he had Carol with him. My heart began to race and my thoughts went wild.

Could Shannon be with them also? Carol came over to me with a big smile on her face and said welcome home. It didn't make any sense why Carol was there and not Shannon. Gus told me when he was sent back to Canada Carol came up a short while after to take care of him.

I asked why Shannon wasn't here and Carol said she couldn't leave because of the shelters. Someone needed to run them and Shannon couldn't trust it to anyone. I wanted to know if all three shelters were still open and Gus said, "Yes, that's the reason she couldn't leave." Carol also said Shannon was being watched by G-men because of her ties with Shamus and Kieran. If Shannon had come up she probably would have been followed.

Mother called for everyone to come to the dining room for food but I stayed behind with Father in the parlor. While alone with Father, he told me he had taken care of everything with the Canadian Government about the situation with the *Black Duck*. Father said after the *Black Duck* was captured Government men from the United States came to Canada to investigate who the boat's owner was. The Canadian Government said the boat had not been registered and they had no records of ownership.

Father also said the Canadian Government told the US investigators that Canada was conducting their own inquiry and wanted the names of the three men who were killed during the capture of the *Black Duck*. Canada said they wanted restitution for the men and that someone was going to have to answer for the deaths. The Coast Guard Board of Investigation declared the captain of the *Black Duck* was at fault for the deaths and pressed no charges against Cornell or the gunner.

I didn't want Captain Cornell or any of his men to be held accountable. I was the one who caused the situation and if anyone had to be punished it should be me. The Canadian Government audited the distillery's books and records to make sure the export taxes were paid. Upon disclosure no charges were brought upon myself or my father. It was ruled that no Canadian laws were broken.

When the birthday party ended and everyone went home I sat with Mother for a little while in the kitchen. She was very angry with me but was happy I was now home and safe. She asked me where I was for the last three months and I told her about Mrs. Myers in Bath, Maine. Mother asked if the news reports were accurate of what happened and I told her yes. She looked at me with disappointment and told me to go to bed and get a good night's rest. We both knew I was at fault and shouldn't have agreed to pick up the liquor from the *Symor*. There was nothing more that needed to be said and after that day Mother never mentioned the incident again.

The following morning I got up early and went to the shed to see if my money was still there. The lock had frozen and the key wouldn't open it. I searched the barn for some tools and found a heavy sledgehammer. After a few good hits the lock broke open and fell into the deep snow at my feet. I opened the crate and all the money was there. I needed to get the cash to the bank so I could repay Mr. Jacobs for his loan.

I went to the distillery to find Gus so he could help me load the crate onto the truck. Father had seen me walking across the road and asked me where I was going. I explained to him how I had taken the money out of the bank and put it in the shed before the stock market crash. He wanted to know how I knew there would be problems with the banking system. When I said Joe had given me the advice Father just shook his head.

Father told me the reason why he didn't want to do business with Joe at the beginning of Prohibition was because he couldn't trust him. Although he had sold Joe whiskey before the laws changed, Father always felt uncomfortable around him and his men. As we walked back to the house Father only said he had hoped I learned a lesson from all this. I told Father I had learned many lessons.

Gus and I moved the crate from the shed to the truck and headed into town. It felt nice to be home again with my family and friends but the feeling had quickly changed. As we pulled into town everyone on the streets stared at us. The people who I thought were my friends kept their distance and no one said anything to us. I asked Gus to stay with the truck and keep an eye on the crate while I met with Mr. Jacobs. When I went into the bank I received the same reception as on the street, just stares.

Mr. Jacobs approached me and asked me to come into his office. We discussed the loan he provided me until I could get back to Blacks Harbour and we also talked about the properties he purchased for me just outside of town. I thanked him for all his help and gave him explicit orders never to tell anyone it was my money being transferred to Boston for Shannon and the shelters. Mr. Jacobs said my secret would always be safe with him.

I filled out the necessary papers to make the deposit and went outside to get Gus and the money. Mr. Jacobs asked that we pull the truck around the back of the bank and he would have one of his tellers help us move the money inside. After the money was placed into the vault, Mr. Jacobs asked me to come back to his office again. Gus and I went inside and sat down in the office. Mr. Jacobs closed the door behind us and then sat at his desk. I don't think Gus had ever been in Mr. Jacobs's office by the way he was acting. Mr. Jacobs asked what I planned to do now that I didn't have the *Black Duck* anymore.

I wasn't sure how to answer the question because I hadn't given it much thought. At that time I didn't know what I wanted to do with my life but I did know I probably wouldn't stay in Blacks Harbour. As Gus and I drove home from town I started to give it more thought. What was I going to do? I couldn't go back to Boston. I had no answers.

That afternoon Mother told me she received a letter from Max. In it, Max said he would be finishing school in a few months and planned to return home. With Max returning to run the businesses there wouldn't be anything for me to do. I had to get my life back in order. I would soon be twenty-two and still had my whole life ahead of me.

Max graduated in the summer of nineteen thirty and after a short trip home went to Europe with his friend Hiram. They visited Hiram's family in Germany and traveled through Spain, France, England, Ireland and Italy. We received letters and postcards from Max at least once a week describing his journeys. Hiram's family tried to convince Max to stay in Europe but Max missed our family and returned home to Canada that November.

Once Max found out what I did he wanted nothing to do with me. We had several quarrels and ended up not speaking to each other. I thought if anyone would understand it would be Max but he told me I would never amount to anything and that I was wasting my life. Max hurt me real bad by what he said and I knew it was time for me to leave home. Max was in charge now and would only make it difficult for me if I did stay.

I signed over the deeds to the properties I purchased outside town to Max thinking it might settle the dispute between us but it didn't. Max said nothing could make up for the disgrace I brought upon our family and especially for the greed which caused men their lives. I tried to explain how I did what I did for all of us so we could keep the distillery running but he didn't want to hear it. His point was right though. What I did was wrong and illegal but it was the adventure I sought, not the money. I knew at that time we might never see each other again.

I spent the next couple of weeks with Gus and Carol and tried to convince them to come back with me to Maine but they already made plans to marry and stay in Blacks Harbour. There, Gus had steady work and Carol wanted to settle down and have children. I wished them both good luck and told them I hoped I would someday see them again.

Just before I left Blacks Harbour Carol gave me a letter she received from Shannon. In the letter Shannon told me she was grateful for all I had done for her and that she would never forget me. She knew I couldn't return to Boston and said she didn't want to leave her sister or the shelters. She had found her place in life and wanted to continue helping the children.

Shannon said Joe had set up a trust fund for the shelters and she was receiving monthly support from him. Shannon had no idea the money was really coming from me although I wanted to tell her. I don't think it would have made a difference; she was going to keep running the shelters no matter what I told her. Now I had no one, not even Shannon. I thought returning to Blacks Harbour after I lost the *Black Duck* would help me get my life back together but it didn't. I had lost everything I ever wanted in just a few short months.

Chapter Twenty-Two

I left Blacks Harbour and returned to Bath in the winter of nineteen thirty. I didn't know where else to go but I knew the shipyard in Bath was always looking for workers. Around that same time the US Coast Guard decided it was time to revamp its fleet of steel ships in order to keep up with the faster rum runners. After confiscating the *Black Duck* the Coast Guard modeled its new cutters after the smaller, faster wooden boats. Specifications were put out to all ship builders to bid on building the faster lightweight boats and the Bath shipyard was awarded the business.

I knew all about building wooden boats and after convincing the superintendent at the shipyard of my experience and skills he hired me immediately. During the next year an a half I lived at Mrs. Myers's house and worked almost every day at the shipyard. Staying busy helped keep my mind off the loss of the *Black Duck* but I never stopped thinking about Shannon. The memories I had of Shannon and someday living our lives together was what kept me going.

Eventually the contract at the shipyard ended with the Coast Guard and I needed to find something else to do. The shipyard superintendent wanted me to stay and work for him on other projects but something inside me said it was time for me to move on. I tried contacting Shannon to see if I could come to Boston to visit her but I was never able to get in touch with her. I wasn't sure if she was just busy or didn't want to see me anymore since I hadn't called or written for almost two years.

After several tries I was able to contact Kieran and asked him if it was safe for me to come to Boston yet. Kieran said it wasn't a good time because the Coast Guard was still looking for the owner of the *Black Duck*. The Coast Guard had a suspicion it might be me because I disappeared around the same time the *Black Duck* was captured. I thought I was all through worrying about the Coast Guard trying to find me but they were being persistent. The Coast Guard wanted to clear their name with the public and the only way they could do that was by bringing me in and getting me to admit it was my fault. I wasn't going to let that happen.

Shortly after my contact with Kieran I received a letter from Gus and Carol. In the envelope with the letter was a newspaper clipping. It was a picture of Shannon and a man named Captain Scully. Peter Scully announced his engagement to Shannon and they planned to move to Westport, Connecticut, after his discharge from the Coast Guard. Scully would help Shannon run the shelters after they were married. The story also said Shannon now had eight shelters between New York and Boston and was going to continue managing them from their new headquarters in Connecticut.

As I continued to read the newspaper clipping it went on to say how Shannon built the business from generous donations and was able to help homeless children everywhere. After receiving the letter from Carol I knew I would never be able to be with Shannon again. Deep inside I wanted to be happy for her but it was such a shock to me. I had gotten over Max being angry with me and losing the *Black Duck* but I wasn't able to get over losing Shannon.

I called Kieran again and asked if he could help me get in touch with Shannon before she got married but he said there was nothing he could do. He told me it would be better for everyone if I just went on and lived my own life without her. I couldn't let Shannon get away from me that easily but I was helpless. If I went back to Boston I may have ended up in jail and I didn't want to stay in Bath anymore.

Soon after receiving the letter from Gus and Carol Mrs. Myers passed away. Mrs. Myers was such a wonderful person and treated me like a son. She had no living relatives and willed her house and all her belongings to me. Now, I was really all alone and had no reason to stay in Bath anymore. I sold Mrs. Myers's house and all her belongings. What I couldn't sell I gave to the local churches along with some of the money from the house. Whatever money was left over I sent to Mr. Jacobs at the bank in Canada. In a letter I asked Mr. Jacobs to send all the proceeds from Mrs. Myers's house to Shannon for the shelters.

I thought about getting another boat and running liquor again but I had no one to buy liquor from since Max was running the distillery now. Plus, I didn't know if Joe, Kieran or Shamus wanted to deal with me anymore. Out of desperation, I called Kieran one more time to see if there was anything I could do for him. Kieran said running liquor on the water was too risky and besides, the Coast Guard had taken possession of the new, faster cutters and it wasn't going to be easy to get close enough to shore to drop the loads.

Kieran told me he had some friends in the Carolinas who could use my help but I would need to be careful and stay out of sight if I could. Kieran said his friends were moonshiners and could be trusted. At that point I didn't trust anyone, not even Kieran. I thought if I just kept moving, eventually the Coast Guard would stop looking for me. Kieran gave me the name and address of his friends and told me he would call them to let them know I would be coming down for a while. Shortly after our conversation I took a train south for the Carolinas.

The southern part of the United States was beautiful but the climate was hot and muggy. I preferred the cooler weather in Canada and Maine but got used to the heat in the South. The beaches were spectacular and the water was always warm. Kieran's friends set me up in a secluded mountainous area and gave me a job as a mechanic in a machine shop. Kieran's friends made a lot of money from running moonshine like me but they dumped it back into making their automobiles fast and elusive. Those Southern boys liked hauling moonshine and running from cops. They made a game out of it.

The moonshiners from Carolina all wanted fast automobiles and they liked racing each other on weekends to see whose was the fastest. I was used to running on water and these guys ran on old dirt roads. That summer the owner of the machine shop, Bill Johnson, purchased a nineteen thirty-three Ford Roadster. It had a leaf spring suspension system and V-8 flathead engine. The automobile was fast out of the dealership but I knew I could make it faster. It was difficult getting traction on the dirt roads so I added extra leaves to the suspension to make it stiffer. The stiffer suspension helped with high-speed cornering and also allowed for more weight to be carried in the trunk. I had lots of fun teaching that crazy moonshiner how to modify his automobile.

Helping Bill and his friends reminded me of the thrill when I installed both Liberty engines in the *Black Duck* and took it out on the ocean for the first time. To these guys, running liquor was all a game because they were running from the cops and making lots of money. They had never seen anyone get killed over liquor and if they had they probably wouldn't have cared.

During the fall of nineteen thirty-three I built a turbo-supercharger and convinced Bill to let me install it on the Ford flathead. He had no idea how much faster it was going to make his car run but after the installation was completed we took the Roadster out for a spin on some back roads. It didn't take me long to show Bill what the car could do with the modification. Bill couldn't believe how much more horsepower the turbo-supercharger made for the flathead V-8. To tell you the truth, even I couldn't believe how much faster it made the automobile go. I knew I had developed something special, but who needed an automobile that fast unless you planned to use it for moving moonshine and running from the cops?

I spent the remainder of the fall fine-tuning the turbo-supercharger for automobiles and built a bunch of spare parts for it. I wasn't sure how reliable it would be because the materials available couldn't withstand the high heat and pressure for too long. I continued making parts from different materials and finally found the right combination of materials to make the turbo-supercharger durable enough for racing. Bill liked what I had done and asked me if I would partner with him to build and sell the turbo-supercharger to other moonshiners, or anyone who wanted to buy it.

Bill and I made a fortune with that bolt on turbo-supercharger design. Once racers found out how reliable they were we were getting orders from all over the country and for all different makes of automobiles. I sent most of my earnings to Mr. Jacobs back in Canada with instructions to keep anonymously funding Shannon's shelters. I often wondered if Shannon knew the money being set to her was really coming from me. Even though I couldn't be with Shannon it was comforting to know I was able to help her financially so she could continue to achieve her dreams.

It was in the winter of nineteen thirty-three and President Roosevelt was ready to end Prohibition. On December third he signed a proclamation declaring the Eighteenth Amendment had been repealed. Eight states enacted the Twenty-First Amendment, which allowed for the manufacture, sale and distribution of alcohol, but it would be controlled by each individual state. Taxation would also be at the state level and needed to be controlled. If the taxes were too high, Europe and Canadian companies would benefit because their governments removed their export tax.

Once I read Prohibition was over I called Max to see how he and the business were doing. Max told me the distillery had more orders than they could handle. He also said the additional farms I bought in Canada had record crops and the farms were now supporting themselves. Because alcoholic beverages were legal in the states the price of wheat, corn, oats, rye and barley all skyrocketed. It was ironic how all of us who made money illegally during the twenties were now prospering in the depression of the thirties.

Max and I had a long talk after that day and settled our

VINCE PISANI

differences. He said I was entitled to some of the profits from the businesses and he wanted to know where to send the money. I told Max to deposit the money in the bank and that Mr. Jacobs would know what to do with it. Max asked me when I was planning to come home again and if I was okay. I told Max about the machine shop and my new partner, Bill. I explained to Max how I developed the turbo-supercharger for automobiles and how well they were selling.

I wasn't sure what Max would say about the new business I started but he told me he thought I would eventually do something with the knowledge I gained from playing around with all the equipment at the farm and distillery. Max wanted to know if I still had plans to go back to school in Boston. I paused for a moment when he said that because my thoughts when back to Shannon. I never did give Max an answer. Besides, I was running a successful business and didn't think I needed to go back to school.

Chapter Twenty-Three

Between nineteen thirty-four and the summer of nineteen thirty-nine I spent most of my time traveling around the southern part of the United States selling my engine components to people interested in racing automobiles. Daytona Beach, Florida, was a frequent stop because a majority of the moonshiners I met in the Carolinas relocated there to race after Prohibition ended. Bill continued to run the machine shop back in North Carolina and shipped the parts our customers ordered to hotels where I stayed so I could deliver them.

Traveling for all those years started to take its toll on me. I hadn't seen Max, my parents or any of my childhood friends in over eight years. I needed to go back to Canada to rest for a while, so I hired a few friends I made during my travels to sell the parts Bill was producing back at the machine shop. Although the parts were selling themselves by word of mouth I still needed someone to show the racers how to install and fine-tune the turbo-superchargers.

Once I set up the new salesmen in Florida I went back to North Carolina to meet with Bill. I told Bill how I missed home and asked him if he would buy out my share of the business. Bill tried to convince me to stay on with the company and said he would set up an engineering department to develop new products and let me run it. I seriously thought about staying with Bill but I really wanted to go home, it was time.

I called home to let Mother and Father know I was planning to return to Canada. Mother was so happy to hear from me that she began to cry on the telephone. Mother said the distillery business had grown to the point where Max couldn't run it by himself anymore. She also said Father and Byron were too old to help and Gus and Carol did what they could but it just wasn't enough.

Mother put Max on the telephone and I let him know I sold my share of the machine shop business and would be home soon. Max didn't say much but I could tell by the sound of his voice he was troubled. Mother was right; although Max had learned much about how to run a business at Harvard he was overwhelmed with all the work. Max wanted to do everything himself and thought he didn't need any help.

When I returned home I could see Max had aged beyond his years. I had to convince Max to take some time off and let me run the businesses for a little while so he could rest. Max was reluctant at first but finally agreed to let me take over the distillery. Shortly after I returned home Max received a letter from his old classmate Hiram. Hiram told how Adolf Hitler was planning to invade neighboring countries and war in Europe was evident.

Hiram asked if he and his family could come to Canada to live with us and work at the distillery. Hiram's family also owned a distillery and knew how to operate the business. Max and I both knew we needed the help so we agreed. I would run the company, Max would get some much needed rest and when Hiram arrived we would share the responsibilities. Max wrote Hiram back and told him to come to Canada.

That summer I spent the time evaluating the business and how it was being run. Byron told me we needed to expand the building but

Max didn't want to. There was not enough space to store the materials we needed to run the business. Max had everything delivered just in time to manufacture but it left us at the hands of our suppliers. If they didn't deliver on time then our business would suffer.

I had a warehouse built adjacent to the existing manufacturing site so we could bring in more bottles. I used my own money to construct the warehouse and never said anything to Max. Once we were able to store more bottles we ran the business twenty-four hours a day. We hired more workers and I finally got everything running real smooth to where we had no more delayed deliveries and no more lost business.

It was early fall and we hadn't heard back from Hiram. Max started to worry but I told him if Hiram needed to sneak his family out of Germany it was better he didn't try to contact us again. On September first Germany invaded Poland. Two days later England and France declared war on Germany. Now, Max and I were really starting to worry about Hiram.

Hiram and his two sisters, Rachel and Anna, finally arrived at our home in mid November. Hiram's parents didn't want to come to Canada because they didn't want to leave their home, business and all their possessions behind. Hiram tried to convince his parents to come but they refused. Hiram's parents said they had lived through a war before and they didn't see any reason to leave.

As much as Hiram wanted to stay with his parents he knew he had to get his sisters out of Europe. Once he left Germany Hiram knew he couldn't return until after the war was over. I don't think I could have left my parents behind if I had to make that decision. After Hiram and his sisters got settled in and Max got the rest he needed, Max, Hiram and I had a meeting to see who would handle responsibilities at the distillery.

We decided Max would run the company and oversee all management positions. I, with the help of Gus, took over all manufacturing and purchasing operations, and Hiram went to work in sales and distribution. Hiram's sister Rachel worked with Carol in the accounting department and Anna worked with Mother at the house to help take care of Father and run errands. We finally had everything under control and with imports of liquor from Europe drastically reduced because of the war, our business continued to grow.

By nineteen forty-one the war became global. On December seventh of that same year Japan attacked Pearl Harbor. It was a big mistake on Japan's part. It thrust the United States into the war. The world was a mess, with fighting going on in Asia, Europe, the Middle East, Africa, and Russia. On April thirtieth, nineteen forty-five, as the allies encroached on Germany, Hitler committed suicide, ultimately ending the war in Europe, Africa, and Russia. Four months after the allies seized Germany the United States dropped an atomic bomb on Japan. A few days after the bomb was dropped Japan surrendered, which ended the war in Asia. The world was finally on its way to peace.

Over the next thirty years our business continued to grow. With Hiram's contacts in Europe we became a large corporation, shipping our liquor everywhere in the world. We were all grateful for our good fortune and I made sure some of the profits we earned went to help rebuild Germany, Hiram's homeland. Hiram returned home but never did find his parents. Max and Rachel married and now have a son and daughter. I, on the other hand, never did marry. I couldn't get Shannon off my mind to have any feelings for another woman.

Carol and Gus have three sons, who are now all grown up. After attending college Gus's three boys returned home to help run the business. Carol and Shannon wrote each other frequently and I learned Shannon had built a new addition to her building in Westport and was planning a commemoration ceremony to honor all those who donated money to help with the homeless children. I came here to Westport to attend the ceremony without Shannon knowing but while I stood in the crowd our eyes met.

I knew she recognized me because the moment she saw me her voice started to shudder as though she was going to cry. I didn't want to ruin her speech or upset her so I left and came here to the bar to get away for a while before I returned home. It was nice seeing Shannon after all these years. Now my life is complete. I could see she still felt something for me.

As the old salty dog finished telling me his story I could see his eyes begin to swell. I didn't know what to say or do for him. The old man had opened my mind to a world I had never known. As I began to think about what to say to thank him he stood up. His body began to lean forward as though he was going to fall so I reached out to grab him. Just as I put my had on his shoulder a beautiful old woman walked up to us and took his hand. She said her name was Shannon and she was there to take him home now.

My friends started to arrive at the bar and I had a feeling it would be the last time I would see that old man. What a great, adventurous life he led. I wanted to know more but the old man's focus had turned from the story to Shannon. As Shannon and the old man turned and began to walk away, I still had lots of questions, so I ran over to that old salty dog, placed my hand on his shoulder, and asked him if that was the end of the story. He paused for a while and as he looked into Shannon's eyes he pulled her close to him and said, "No, it's the beginning of a new one."

The End